THE HARD TIME BUNCH

Center Point
Large Print

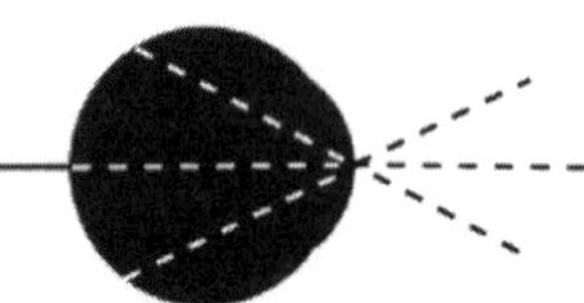

THE HARD TIME BUNCH

Clifton Adams

Center Point Publishing
Thorndike, Maine

This Center Point Large Print edition
is published in the year 2010 by arrangement with
Golden West Literary Agency.

The text of this Large Print edition is unabridged.
In other aspects, this book may vary
from the original edition.
Printed in the United States of America
on permanent paper.
Set in 16-point Times New Roman type.

ISBN: 978-1-60285-782-7

Library of Congress Cataloging-in-Publication Data

Adams, Clifton.
The hard time bunch / Clifton Adams. — Center Point large print ed.
p. cm.
ISBN 978-1-60285-782-7 (lib. bdg. : alk. paper)
1. Large type books. I. Title.
PS3551.D34H29 2010
813′.54—dc22

2010001372

CHAPTER ONE

Frank Beeler had come a long way with little real hope of getting the job. For one thing, the newspaper had been a week old by the time he discovered the advertisement. For another, he had begun to doubt his ability to hold a job, in the unlikely event that one should fall his way.

The hotel clerk regarded him with a jaded eye. Almost before Beeler could say what was on his mind, the prim little man snapped, "Sit down somewhere. I'll let you know when Mr. Keating can see you."

"Is there somebody else waitin' to see him?"

The clerk looked at him with icy disbelief. "Over there. All of them." His tone suggested that the management, by allowing such men in the lobby of the Travelers Hotel, was guilty of grave folly, at the very least, and probably something much worse. Beeler took a seat on a leather-covered couch and quietly observed the other hopefuls. He had to admit there was some justification for the clerk's attitude; they were a dull-eyed, depressed, and depressing bunch. The aura of defeat hovered in their corner of the hotel lobby like thunderheads in April.

And I am one of them, Beeler thought to himself. Lord help me.

From time to time the clerk would motion to one

of them. The man would tramp up the stairs, hat in hand, and in a few minutes he would tramp back down again, the stamp of hopelessness on his face. Noontime came and went, but none of the men made any move to go to dinner. Probably, like Beeler, they had no money for cafe food. They sat passively, staring blankly into space. A few of them wore shapeless suits of cheap wool and cotton material, but most of them wore rough jeans and flannel shirts and heavy brogan shoes. They might as well have been carrying signs, Beeler thought, with "Sodbuster" printed in red letters.

Every few minutes one of the men would slip a tattered newspaper out of his pocket and carefully read the advertisement, as if to reassure himself that he was in the right place. Beeler knew it by heart. WANTED, MAN TO GUIDE HUNTING PARTY THROUGH EASTERN INDIAN TERRITORY. MUST BE FAMILIAR WITH THE LAND AND CAPABLE OF DEALING WITH INDIANS IF NECESSARY. GOOD PAY TO THE RIGHT MAN. ENQUIRE MR. KEATING, TRAVELERS HOTEL, OKLAHOMA CITY.

Good pay to the right man. Beeler smiled a trifle grimly. During the past year he had watched the last of his savings melt away. He had killed two mules trying to break the tough prairie sod of his quarter section. Sometimes he thought he was on the verge of killing himself.

What did he have to show for it? A half-dug-out

sod hut, a small cleared field where seed corn rotted in the ground, and an aching back. He had run out of money four months ago and credit shortly after that. If it hadn't been for Elizabeth he would have left the place long ago. A hard winter and two blistering summers, with little rain in between, had about convinced him that he would never make a farmer.

Beeler sat back and thought about Elizabeth. Strangely, he had trouble remembering just what she looked like, except that she had quite a lot of long blond hair which she was inordinately proud of. And graceful hands. And serious blue eyes. If things had gone well they would have been married by this time.

"Mr. Beeler," the little desk clerk announced grudgingly, "Mr. Keating will see you now. Room 212."

"Much oblige," Beeler told him gravely and climbed the stairs to the second floor. The Travelers, according to world hotel standards, was probably a fourth-rate establishment at best. But in Oklahoma City, a town which had not existed fifteen months ago, it passed as a place of almost sinful luxury. There were wool rugs on the floors, pictures in ornate frames on the walls, as well as a great deal of polished brass, painted china lamps, and black oak furniture. Having just come from his dirt-floored sod hut on the North Canadian, Beeler was impressed.

He found 212 and knocked on the dark oak door. An impatient voice ordered him to come inside.

Beeler stepped into what was actually a rather shabby, vulgarly furnished room—but to a man who had for more than a year shared his mud hut with spiders and rattlesnakes, it was as grand as a palace. The object of Beeler's trip to Oklahoma City—Duane Francis Keating—sat at a small desk in the center of the room. He wrote something on a sheet of paper and asked sharply, "Name?"

"Beeler. Frank Beeler."

Mr. Keating jotted the name down. "Occupation?"

"Now or before?"

Keating was in his middle twenties, immaculately groomed in crisp linens and soft English woolens, with a silky little mustache drooping sullenly at the corners of his mouth. He lifted his head and scowled. "What do you mean, now or before?"

"Now I'm tryin' to be a farmer," Beeler told him frankly, "and not havin' too much luck with it. Before that, I rode for the court at Fort Smith."

The young man blinked. "The court?"

"The federal one. I worked as a field deputy to the marshal there."

"Ahh," Keating said, smiling faintly. "You were a United States deputy marshal."

"That's right. But I quit to make the land run last year when they opened the Oklahoma country."

"How long did you work as a deputy marshal?"

"Five years, off and on."

"Off and on?"

"Once I was laid up with the fever. Another time with a bullet in my leg."

"I see." Mr. Duane Francis Keating sat back in his chair, crossed his arms on his beautifully tailored vest, and favored Beeler with a petulant smile. "What made you apply for a job as a hunting guide, Mr. Beeler?"

Beeler shrugged. "I need the money. And from the sound of your advertisement, I think I could do the work. I know some Creek and Choctaw. A few words of Cherokee. If you're pressed for time maybe I could save you a few days in gettin' your permits."

Keating looked blank. "Permits?"

"To hunt in Indian country. You have to get permission from the government of whatever nation you're in. I could do that for you without any trouble."

Keating still looked slightly puzzled, as though he had never heard of permits before. "I think you'd better talk to Mr. Conmy and Mr. Sutter," he said slowly.

"Are they goin' on the hunt too?"

Keating smiled in a peculiar way. "It's *their* hunt. From beginning to end. I'll be along as a . . . hired hand, like yourself. If you get the job."

Beeler had the pleasant feeling that maybe his

luck was beginning to turn. “That’s fine with me. Let’s talk to Conmy and Sutter.”

“One moment.” Keating added several lines of writing to the paper. “How much would you expect to be paid for your services, in the event that Mr. Conmy and Mr. Sutter find you acceptable?”

“How long will the party last?”

“Two weeks, I should say. Possibly longer.”

Beeler did some rapid figuring. Two weeks at two dollars a day would come to almost thirty dollars. Only a new homesteader in Oklahoma Territory, in that year of 1890, would appreciate the magnificence of such a sum. It would allow him to re-establish his credit—for a little while, at least. However, he thought, in hard pursuit of his fantasy, if thirty dollars was magnificent, forty-five dollars would be riches almost beyond the imagination of a common sodbuster.

He took a deep breath and said quickly, “Three dollars a day and expenses.”

Keating’s mouth twitched in a quietly superior smile. “I don’t think Mr. Conmy or Mr. Sutter will be inclined to quibble with that figure.”

They left Keating’s room, walked down the carpeted corridor to number 228, a corner room. Keating knocked.

Beeler stood patiently in the hallway, his arms folded, quietly admiring a gilt-framed mirror on the wall. With a smile, he thought of the broken and scaling bit of looking glass above the washstand in his sod hut on the North Canadian.

On the other side of number 228's door there seemed to be a party of some kind going on. There was a good deal of loud talking and masculine laughter. And once they heard a titter which was definitely feminine. Beeler began to think that maybe this was not the best time to interrupt Mr. Conmy and Mr. Sutter in whatever it was they were doing. But Keating, after a brief pause, knocked a second time.

On the other side of the door all sound stopped. Beeler stared at the door while some rather bizarre thoughts went through his mind. At last an irritable male voice asked, "Who is it?"

"It's Keating, Warren. I have a Mr. Frank Beeler with me; I think you ought to talk to him."

"A Mr. Frank Beeler," the voice on the other side of the door echoed, imitating Keating's precise enunciation. It was not a very good imitation because the voice in room 228 was somewhat thickened by liquor—but it was enough to evoke a muffled chuckle and a feminine giggle. It was enough to cause Keating's face to go strangely pale—but he only said, "May we come in, Warren?"

"You first." Conmy sounded amused. "Ask Mr. Beeler to wait a minute."

With the air of a man who was prepared for any eventuality, Keating nodded for Beeler to wait in the corridor. He entered the room and closed the door behind him. After perhaps two minutes he opened the door again and motioned for Beeler to step inside.

Halfway across the threshold Beeler froze. He stood so still that the blood seemed to stop flowing in his veins. It had been so long since he had faced the violent end of a gun that he had almost forgotten what a frightening experience it could be. His stomach seemed to shrink to the size of a small, hard nut. His legs were like rags.

The sensation of overwhelming fear lasted only for an instant. Reason told him that the two men who were grinning at him over the sights of their rifles could not possibly be interested in killing him. A darting glance at their slack faces, and the nearly empty bourbon bottle on the dresser, told him that this was merely their idea of a hilarious prank. Also, there was the smell of gun oil in the air. He glimpsed cleaning rods and rags on the bed, as well as several rounds of cleaned cartridges. So they were not complete fools—at least they had sense enough to keep their rifles in order. Probably the rifles weren't even loaded.

Probably. But it was the rare lawman who lasted five years in the field on the strength of probabilities.

The two men widened their grins. They began slowly to squeeze the triggers.

The rifle muzzles were less than twelve inches

from Beeler's face; he smelled oil and steel and the memory of burnt powder. On the edge of the bed a young woman watched the scene with a smile that suggested both boredom and amusement. Beeler did not see her. He saw only the muzzles of the two rifles and the two fingers leisurely squeezing the triggers.

Suddenly the hammers fell with twin metallic thuds, and with them, Beeler felt sure, went years of his life.

The man called Conmy suddenly burst into howls of laughter. Both he and the second man, Sutter, flung their rifles on the bed and doubled in helpless convulsions of mirth. They gurgled and sputtered and roared until tears streamed from their eyes. They fell into chairs, gasping for breath, still laughing uproariously. They continued to laugh until they were reduced to babbling, gasping heaps.

Through it all, the woman on the edge of the bed merely smiled absently and regarded them with tolerance and affection. Keating stood just inside the doorway, waiting patiently, with the air of a man who had witnessed such behavior many times before.

"You . . . you ought to have seen your face!" Conmy managed through fits and starts of waning merriment.

"White as a bedsheet!" Sutter gurgled, sounding as if he were slowly being strangled.

"When you first saw the rifle muzzles in your face!"

"When you saw the hammers start to fall!"

Beeler watched them for some time without making a sound. The inside of his mouth felt dry and gritty. His throat was constricted and aching. He knew that if he had tried to speak at that moment his words would come out a thin squeak. So he concentrated on breathing steadily in and out while waiting for the fury to cool inside him.

"What did you say your name was?" Conmy asked at last. Both he and Sutter had white handkerchiefs in their hands, dabbing at their eyes.

When Beeler still made no sound, Conmy took from his pocket the information that Keating had so carefully written down. "Your name is Frank Beeler. You speak some Creek and Choctaw and a little Cherokee, and you used to be a United States deputy marshal." The two men dabbed a last time at their reddened eyes and put their handkerchiefs away. "Keating, get Mr. Beeler a glass and pour him some whiskey. He looks as if he could use a drink."

There was nothing that Beeler could think of at that moment that he needed more than a strong drink. But he shook his head when Keating offered him the glass.

Conmy began chuckling again. "It was just a little joke, Beeler," he said comfortably. "You're not a man who can't take a joke, are you?"

"It depends," Beeler said stiffly, when he was sure that he could speak. He could feel that his shirt was plastered with sweat to his shoulders. His stomach fluttered nervously. He thought how hugely satisfying it would be to step quietly forward and, without another word, throw his fist into the middle of Mr. Conmy's grinning face.

But would it be forty-five dollars worth of satisfaction? After a moment's hesitation, he decided that it wouldn't. He merely looked at Conmy and said, "Tell you the truth, I'm not much good at jokin' with guns."

"Well . . . ," Conmy said generously, "maybe it wasn't such a good idea after all. I apologize. So does Mr. Sutter, I'm sure."

Beeler nodded. Maybe it was going to be all right. Maybe, after a shaky start, he'd get the job and renew his credit in time for a late planting. Maybe he could even convince Elizabeth Stans that he was capable of doing something besides tracking down outlaws. "Let's just forget it," he said, and suddenly the room was free of electricity.

Conmy sat back and smiled, but this time it was a businesslike smile. "Good, then we'll get started with the introductions. I'm Warren Conmy. The lady over there"—he smiled at the young woman—"is my wife. The gentleman there is my brother-in-law, Ben Sutter. I believe you've already met my secretary, Mr. Keating."

Beeler glanced with mild interest at Keating—the only secretaries he knew worked for the court; he had never met a man like Conmy who had one all to himself. He nodded to the others, noting briefly that both men were about Keating's age, in their middle twenties. They were dressed almost alike, in expensive suits of Bedford cord and black-tooled boots. They even looked alike—enough alike to be brothers instead of merely brothers-in-law. Mrs. Conmy, like her brother and her husband, bore the mark of quality, good breeding, and probably a pampered childhood. She sat comfortably erect, fair and beautiful, smiling coolly at Beeler.

While Conmy studied the paper that Keating had given him, Ben Sutter settled back in his chair and, dangling one foot over the arm, lazily lit a cigar. Nobody asked Beeler to sit down. It was obvious that, in the world of the Conmys and the Sutters, the hired help was expected to know its place. Well—Beeler shrugged to himself—for a renewed line of credit he didn't mind being reasonably respectful.

Conmy looked up from the paper. "Why did you quit your job as deputy marshal? You *did* quit, didn't you? They didn't have to let you go for some reason?"

"You can check with the chief marshal at Fort Smith if you want to. I quit because the pay was too low and the chances of getting killed were too high." He didn't figure that his plans to marry Elizabeth Stans were any of Conmy's business.

"Are you afraid of getting killed?"

To Beeler, the question didn't seem to deserve a direct answer, so he said, "Ain't you?"

Ben Sutter chuckled and flicked cigar ash on the floor. "Got you there, Warren."

Warren Conmy ignored him and looked again at the paper. "Keating mentioned something about permits. What's that about?"

"Commercial hunters have been goin' into the Nations and cleaned out the game. The Indians want to put a stop to it. You have to get permission from the tribal council if you want to hunt. And you can't ship out any of the game you kill. Not even if you're an Indian."

"How long will it take to get one of these permits?"

"A day—maybe two. What are you huntin' for?"

A curious blankness came over the faces of the two young men. "We thought we'd like to go down to the Choctaw country," Conmy said slowly. "There are mountains there, I hear, that not many white men have ever seen."

"Unless you're an outlaw runnin' from the deputy marshals. What did you want to hunt for in the mountains?"

Ben Sutter blew a cloud of smoke toward the ceiling. "What do you suggest?"

This seemed like a strange question to Beeler.

Obviously they had gone to a great deal of trouble to arrange this hunting party—now it looked like they didn't even know what they wanted to go after. Still, he guessed that the sons of rich families like the Conmys and Sutters were used to doing about as they pleased, on whatever whim that happened to come to them. "Well," he said, "there's deer, of course. Maybe some elk. Panthers and bobcats and a few brown bears. Plenty of coons and possum and turkeys and wolves."

Mrs. Conmy, looking as if the conversation was beginning to bore her, got up and went to the window and stared down at the raw, new town of Oklahoma City. Conmy and Sutter sat quite still for a while, looking at each other. At last Sutter smiled and said, "Wolves, I think."

Then Conmy also smiled and nodded, "Yes, wolves."

Mentally, Beeler shrugged. If they wanted to go for wolves when they had fair chances at panthers and bears, it was their business. "All right, have you got your own dogs?"

"Dogs?" Conmy looked surprised.

"They run wolves with dogs. That's the way we hunt them out here."

The two men got that look again. "It's not the way *we* hunt them," Sutter said.

Conmy said, "No, forget the dogs. We won't need them."

To Beeler the whole point of hunting wolves was watching and listening to the dogs. However, he guessed that they did things differently where the Conmys and Sutters came from, wherever that was. "All right," he said agreeably, "we'll forget the dogs. How much gear will you be packin'?"

"Only what's necessary," Conmy said offhandedly. "We'll leave it up to you to get things together." As an afterthought he added, "We'll want a tent of some sort, of course, for Mrs. Conmy and myself. And one for Ben and Mr. Keating, and whatever you need for yourself." He thought for a moment. "And we'll need the necessary cooking equipment—Mrs. Conmy is rather particular about the food she eats."

Beeler sighed to himself. "Mrs. Conmy will be coming with us then?"

"Of course she will come with us; did you think I'd leave her here?"

"Do you have anybody special in mind to put up the tents, and take them down, and pack them, and unpack them, while doin' the cookin' in between?"

Conmy smiled. "Yes, I have someone in mind. Don't worry, Beeler, you won't be asked to do anything but guide us."

"Then I've got the job?"

Conmy and Sutter nodded together, but Conmy was again the spokesman. "Yes. We are not complete fools, Mr. Beeler. Our little joke when you first came in wasn't really a joke after all. We were curious to see how you controlled your temper under . . . provocation. We assumed that you had a reasonable amount of nerve and were capable of doing what was asked of you, or you wouldn't have lasted long as a deputy marshal."

Indirectly, he was saying that they had wanted to know how desperate Beeler was for money. Well, now they knew that he was desperate enough to take a good scare and hold his temper. What good that knowledge did them, Beeler couldn't guess.

There was a quick one-two knock at the door and Conmy said, "It's unlocked, Hump, come on in."

A big man with a shining pink face and little blue button eyes stumped into the room on a wooden leg. The peg leg thudded with hammer-like blows as he maneuvered to close the door behind him. Then he stood for a moment looking at Beeler, sizing him up without expression, like a Bourbon Street gambler looking at his hole card. He was dressed neatly and expensively, as was everyone in the room, with the exception of Beeler. Even the peg leg, neatly fitted just below the left knee, shone with a kind of polished elegance. Beeler, in his self-patched flannel shirt and his threadbare California pants, began to feel like an outcast among the hired help.

"Hump," Conmy was saying easily, "meet Mr.

Frank Beeler. He's going to guide us on our hunt. Mr. Beeler, this is Mr. Humphrey O'Toole."

That took care of "Hump" and the introductions. Beeler guessed that the man with the glowing face and peg leg was some kind of Conmy servant, like Keating, but apparently Conmy didn't consider it necessary to go into explanations. One thing about O'Toole that attracted Beeler's attention, even more than the beetlike face and wooden leg, was the obvious bulge on the left side of his suit coat, about the kind of bulge a .38-caliber double-action revolver, in a shoulder holster, would make. A strange kind of weapon, Beeler thought to himself, to be taking on a hunting trip.

The next two days were busy ones for Beeler. By telegraph he arranged for Creek and Choctaw hunting permits. From a variety of places he got together saddle and pack animals, with appropriate rigs, two slightly used army dog tents, necessary sleeping gear, and basic food items. O'Toole took care of the fancy cooking equipment and supplies. He also accumulated, somehow, six bottles of French brandy, one case of red burgundy wine, a carton each of fresh garlic and shallots, a large sack of dried Italian mushrooms, several small cans of black French truffles, and whole goose livers, six pounds of unsalted butter (which would go rancid after the first day), one half gallon of olive oil, a whole Virginia ham, cured to rocklike hardness, and three cases of canned goods that Beeler didn't have the heart to look at.

"Two years ago," Beeler told Conmy, "a party of army officers, a Russian duke and his family, as well as all kinds of government bigwigs, went out on a monthlong huntin' trip, and they never carried half this much stuff with them!"

Conmy only laughed. "They didn't have a woman like my wife with them, or they would have."

"It's goin' to take six pack horses just to carry the stuff that O'Toole's rustled up."

"Then get us six pack horses; there's no arguing with Mrs. Conmy about these things." It was late on the second day and they were preparing to leave early the next morning. Warren Conmy, Mrs. Conmy—whose name was Verna—and Ben Sutter were together in the hotel room which they rarely left. Conmy and Sutter were engaged in what Beeler had learned was their favorite pastime, gambling. It didn't matter what kind of gambling, as long as the stakes were high and the action fast—today they were throwing knives at a mark on the black oak door.

They were heavy fighting knives, with blood gutters and tilted tips, and the door was shattered beyond the wildest hope of repair. This didn't seem to bother the two young sportsmen. On the dresser were two stacks of greenbacks; after each throw the winner would take one greenback from the other's stack. They were betting twenty dollars on each throw, and Sutter was the winner by almost three hundred dollars.

"I wonder," Beeler said dryly, "if you've given any thought to what the hotel manager's goin' to say when he sees the shape his door's in?"

Sutter laughed. "Nothing much, I imagine. The winner will buy him a new door."

Verna Conmy, as she almost always did, sat on the edge of the bed reading a magazine. From time to time she would glance up and smile tolerantly at her husband and her brother. "Don't pay any attention to them," she told Beeler. "They only want to be noticed. They've been behaving like this from the time they were children."

"Then I guess you've all known each other for a long while," Beeler said.

"Lord, how long!" Ben Sutter sighed. Lazily, he flipped his knife, and the point thudded into the ace of hearts that Conmy had fixed to the door. "How many head-to-head poker games! How many wrestling matches, and brawls, and footraces!"

"And boxing," Warren Conmy said, slamming his own knife into the door beside Sutter's.

"And the time I killed the hartebeest with a pistol."

"And I bet you ten to one that you couldn't. That's why you remember all those times so well, you always win."

Beeler had no idea what a hartebeest was, but he knew that to kill any sort of animal with a pistol took an expert's eye and nerve. Beeler was about to say as much when he became aware of the uneasy silence in the room. The Conmys and Ben Sutter looked at each other sheepishly, as though talking about themselves in front of a stranger was something to be slightly ashamed of. Then Conmy got up briskly and pulled the knives out of the door. "Well, I expect you've got plenty to do, Beeler, if we're to get started tomorrow morning."

"Enough," Beeler told him, recognizing the tone of dismissal. "I'll meet you at first light at the wagon yard on South Broadway."

Over Humphrey O'Toole's violent objections Beeler discarded some of the camping equipment that he considered useless. It was enough that they were packing a coal-oil camp stove and five gallons of fuel, not to mention a sizable mountain of fancy foodstuffs and liquor, without which people like the Sutters and the Conmys would find life not worth living. Even so, it took four pack horses to carry what O'Toole considered to be absolute necessities.

They caused a considerable stir as they rode up Broadway in the cool of that August morning. Beeler, feeling slightly ridiculous, led the way, with Verna Conmy at his side. Mrs. Conmy was elegant as always, regal in her black cord riding dress and small black hat. On her livery sidesaddle, atop a rented gray gelding, she rode past the gawking townsmen like a medieval queen passing through a gathering of thunderstruck peasants. Conmy and Sutter lagged behind a way, smiling sleepily at the citizens who had come out on the sidewalk to watch the procession. Keating and Humphrey O'Toole brought up the drag with the pack animals.

A short distance up North Broadway the new town of Oklahoma City suddenly ended. They crossed the Santa Fe tracks and took a section-line road to the east. Beeler expected to be in Creek country before nightfall.

CHAPTER TWO

Leo Brannon had personally scouted the Katy tracks from the North Fork of the Canadian to the northern boundary of the Creek Nation, and this was the spot that he had settled on. It was, in Leo's opinion, the best place he had ever seen for robbing a train.

"Boys," he said proudly to the rest of the bunch, "if there was ever a place to pull a first-class holdup, this here's it!"

What was left of the Brannon bunch—Babe Brannon, John Coyotesong, and Rafe Jackson—stood on the embankment beside their leader. What Leo had said was true; it looked like an ideal place to hold up a train. But there was a remarkable lack of enthusiasm in their faces. They were thinking of other places which had seemed almost as ideal as this one, where their efforts had ended in disaster. They were thinking of the little place outside of McAlester's, in the Choctaw Nation. In a convenient gunsight defile, like this one, they had stopped the train all right, but at the crucial moment the engineer had simply backed up onto a trestle where they could not get at it. That was the time Red Luffy took a bullet through his gun hand and decided to look for another line of work.

"I know what you're thinkin'," Leo said heartily, seeing the sour expression on their faces.

"But we learned a thing or two at McAlester's. Now we know better'n to stop a train at one end and let it go at the other. Look down there." He pointed to the north to where the gleaming tracks converged in the narrow pass. "Did you ever see anything prettier'n that? All we got to do is roll a big rock on the tracks, and there she is, caught like a balky steer in a brandin' chute!"

It sounded easy, the way Leo told it. The trouble was, all the jobs sounded easy the way Leo told them—including the one in Kansas where Patty Simms had blown himself up trying to open a safe with faulty dynamite. Or the time in the Cherokee Nation when, in a brush with the Indian Light Horse, Roy Pugh had taken a bullet in the leg and decided he'd rather not be an outlaw after all.

They were a hard time bunch. Farm boys for the most part, but hard times and two bone-dry summers had forced them off their sterile quarter sections. And hard times had followed them into their new profession, which was robbing trains. Or *would* be, just as soon as they managed to bring off a successful holdup.

"Boys," Leo Brannon, the eternal optimist, was telling them now, "this time we can't miss. We got the train, we got the place . . . and we know just what we're goin' after!" He sighed blissfully. "Forty thousand dollars!"

They thought about it for a while and had to

admit that it did have a nice ring. *Forty thousand dollars!*

Babe Brannon, the younger of the two brothers and something of a cynic, said dryly, "I still ain't crazy about the notion of everything comin' so easy. From what I've seen of train robbin', nothin's ever as easy as it looks. Take that bird in Baxter Springs as a sample."

His older brother looked indignant. They were both gangling, rawboned men in their middle thirties, with the stamp of failure in their weathered faces. The thing that made them different was that Leo had not yet learned to accept the obvious fact that he was a failure; he was exasperated that his younger brother could never seem to see the brighter side of things. "That bird in Baxter Springs," he told Babe impatiently, "is the luckiest thing that's happened to us since the dry-up run us off our farm. He's a big muck-a-muck with the Free State Feed and Grain Company; he showed us that card with the printin' on it to prove it."

"If he's such a big muck-a-muck with the company, how come he wants us to rob it?"

"It ain't *his* company we'll be robbin', it's the *insurance* company. Babe, can't you get anything straight at all?"

Insurance—to Leo, as well as to Babe—was a new and hopelessly abstruse concept. Leo had accepted it on faith that there *was* such a thing. According to the feed-company man, the company's loss would be made good by the insurance company, which was why he had come to the bunch with his robbery scheme. "This," he had explained to them, "is the way it works. The feed company is shippin' the money by railroad express to some ranchers in Texas, in payment for some cattle they trailed for us. The money is insured by this big company in Boston. So when you boys hold up the train it won't hardly be like stealin' at all. The feed company won't lose anything, and neither will the ranchers. Nobody loses anything. Except for that big insurance company back East, and they already got more money than they know what to do with."

At this point the feed-company man—whose name was Bertrand Blinn—smiled slyly. "But the prettiest thing of all about my scheme is this: the robbery can be pulled off with absolute safety, with no risk whatsoever to anybody!"

This argument had had a powerful appeal to Rafe Jackson and John Coyotesong, as well as Leo Brannon. But Babe Brannon had remained suspicious. "I'd be right interested to know," he had told Blinn, "how a body could rob a train in absolute safety."

The feed-company man had beamed at them. "Easiest thing in the world," he assured them with a wide grin. "If the express agent on the train happens to be an old pal, like this one is, of mine."

It had sounded perfect, and it still did to Leo.

After the robbery the outlaws would divide the forty thousand dollars with Mr. Bertrand Blinn, and the feed company and the ranchers would recover their money from the insurance company. Everybody would gain and nobody would be the loser. Except, of course, the insurance company, which hardly counted.

"Boys," Mr. Bertrand Blinn had assured them, "this will be the easiest train robbery in the history of railroadin'. All you got to do is find a place to stop the train. My pal in the express car will take care of the rest."

"Well," Leo now told his followers, "here's the place. And tomorrow's the day. In less'n twenty-four hours we'll all be rich men—what do you think about *that?*"

Rafe Jackson grinned self-consciously. He, like the two brothers, was a poor farm boy and was slightly stunned by the prospect of such riches. John Coyotesong, a barrel-chested, bandy-legged little Comanche, merely shrugged. In his thirty-five years he had lived first in the red man's world, then the white man's world, and he had come to the conclusion that they were both overrated.

At two o'clock that afternoon, they watched the train huffing contentedly between the rolling green hills of the Creek Nation. It entered the gun-sight defile, laying down a rolling streamer of black smoke. "Right *there,*" Leo Brannon said, grinning happily, "is where she stops! The engineer'll see the boulder on the tracks and throw on the brakes. Back there at the tail end of the train John and Rafe will roll down another boulder. No backin' away from us *this* time and playin' fancy till a posse comes! John, have you and Rafe got everything straight?"

The little Comanche looked unhappy. "Thee are loco," he grumbled. "Why don't thee rip up the track and be done with it?" As a boy, John Coyotesong had attended the agency school—English, as taught by Quaker teachers and spoken by a Quahada Comanche was apt to take a stranger by surprise when he first heard it.

"We ain't goin' to rip up the tracks," Leo told him patiently, "because then there would be a wreck and somebody would most likely get theirselves hurt, or maybe killed, and what do you reckon *that* would do for us? I'll tell you what—it would get us hung. Robbin' a train's one thing—even the railroad expects to get robbed once in a while. But killin' . . ." He shook his shaggy head. "No, sir, there ain't goin' to be no killin' in this outfit if I can help it."

They watched the train climb the long grade out of the pass. Besides the locomotive and coal car there were three passenger coaches, the express car, four boxcars, and a caboose. It looked as harmless as a string of sodbuster wagons returning from a Saturday visit to a country store.

"Yes, sir," the gang leader said with impressive confidence, "this time tomorrow we're all goin' to be rich men!"

By noon of the next day they had everything ready. One huge sandstone boulder was already on the tracks. John Coyotesong and Rafe Jackson had another one teetering on the embankment, ready with pry poles to dump it onto the tracks when Leo gave the word. In the distance they could hear the heavy breathing of the Katy locomotive.

Leo Brannon checked his rifle for the dozenth time that day. Not, he kept telling himself, that he meant to use it. Robbing trains, he was convinced, could be as non-violent as clerking in a general store—it all depended on how a person went about it.

They could see the smoke rising above the wooded hills. Leo looked at his brother, Babe, and grinned. "Can't nothin' go wrong this time, Babe."

Babe shrugged. "Maybe. But I'd be easier in my mind if I had more trust in Mr. Bertrand Blinn."

Leo made an exasperated sound. It was an old story with the two brothers; Leo was always sure that things would work out fine, and Babe was sure that everything would go smash. Leo considered it pure contrariness on his brother's part that Babe usually managed to be right.

About two hundred yards down the embankment Rafe Jackson began waving his hat and hollering. "Here she comes! Here she comes!" Leo, just as glad to have the long-standing argument interrupted, broke into a wide grin. "Get ready with that pry pole!" he hollered back. By that time the black cowcatcher of the locomotive had nosed into the pass.

The engine sounded like a big, fat old man who had just climbed a few steps to the dinner table. It huffed along contentedly. Leo thought he could detect a sound of friendliness in the wheezing and hissing of the steam. He considered this a good omen.

Suddenly the engineer saw the boulder on the tracks; instantly he put on the brakes and the entire train shuddered violently. There was a din of crashing metal as the iron couplings came together. Already the engineer had guessed what had happened and was trying desperately to put the locomotive in reverse.

"Let 'er go!" Leo Brannon hollered to Rafe Jackson and John Coyotesong.

The great sandstone boulder wobbled forward, uncertainly at first, but quickly picking up speed as it started down the embankment. The huge rock struck the iron platform at the rear of the caboose and settled between the tracks. Leo Brannon laughed out loud to see how perfectly his plan was working. "All right, boys, go to it!"

The four outlaws put their horses down the

embankment, firing a few shots in the air just to let the trainmen know they meant business. Babe Brannon made for the locomotive and ordered the engineer and the fireman down to the ground. Rafe Jackson headed toward the rear of the train and rounded up the brakeman. Leo and John Coyotesong tied their horses to the iron landing of the first passenger coach.

The two outlaws entered the coach grinning good-naturedly at the bug-eyed passengers. "Nobody starts any trouble and nobody gets hurt," Leo promised them.

One young bravo started to rise indignantly, but John Coyotesong shoved the muzzle of his .45 in his face and said, "Thee sit down." The startled passenger dropped like a stone into his seat and did not move again.

The outlaws moved to the second coach and found the conductor hiding behind the water cooler. It didn't take much talking to convince him that it would be better for everybody concerned if he would circulate from one coach to the other and keep the passengers quiet.

John Coyotesong was eyeing with considerable interest a large diamond ring on the finger of one of the female passengers. Leo took his arm and said sternly, "None of that! The fewer folks we get sore at us, the better off we'll be. Our business today is between us and that insurance company in Boston."

Personally, John would have settled for the diamond ring and a few gold watches. On the other hand, a Comanche didn't desert the leader of a war party in the middle of a raid. Reluctantly, he left the ring where it was.

Leo left John inside the coach to watch the passengers. Babe was waiting for him at the bottom of the landing. "Rafe's herdin' the trainmen down by the caboose. What about the passengers?"

"A bunch of women, dudes, and drummers," Leo told him. "They'll set quiet, but I left John with them, just in case. Have you talked to the express agent yet?"

"I was waitin' for you." They crunched along the cinder-strewn siding to the express coach. A pleasant-looking young man with an easy smile and a beautiful head of wavy hair tossed them a little salute.

"You boys're the Brannons, I guess," he said. "Mr. Blinn said to watch out for you. I'm Jack Ford."

"Well, Mr. Ford," Leo said to him, "what else did Mr. Blinn tell you?"

The agent chuckled. "All business, ain't you? Well, I guess that's the best way to be when you're holdin' up a train." He chuckled again. "I guess you boys've had some experience in your line, but I'd like to ask you somethin'. Have you ever been on a holdup before that went as slick as this one?"

"That depends," Babe told him suspiciously. "We ain't got nothin' out of this one yet."

"You have now," agent Ford told him happily. He shoved a heavy iron box into the doorway of the express car.

The Brannons shot anxious looks up and down the track to make sure none of the trainmen or passengers was watching. "Damnation!" Babe said, shaking his head. "We can't pack a thing like that with us. Have you got a key to unlock it?"

"The only key's at the money's destination, in Texas."

"Then we'll have to shoot it open."

Agent Ford seemed to find something alarming in that suggestion. "Boys," he said quickly, "I'll tell you the truth, I'd like to get this wound up with as little fuss as possible. Why don't you put your ropes on that box and drag it off a piece? When the train pulls out you can open it any way you feel like."

To Babe Brannon this sounded like a strange request. He was about to say as much when a woman in the passenger coach began to scream.

Leo groaned. "John's got his eye on that ring again!" He stared distractedly at the strongbox. "Hell," he complained, "we can't go draggin' a thing like that cross country like it was a piece of firewood!"

"Have one of the boys cut a pair of drag poles," Jack Ford suggested. "Like an Indian travois."

The outlaw leader flapped his arms in irritation. He couldn't see the sense of going to all the trouble of cutting drag poles, but he supposed that the express agent knew what he was talking about. "Well," he said grudgingly, "I guess it won't take long. Babe, you get the poles cut while I see what all the racket's about." He raced up the line of cars and hollered into the passenger coach. "John, what the hell's goin' on in there?"

The little Comanche appeared on the top landing. "Woman's loco," he said indifferently. In his hand he was holding a gleaming four-pound fighting knife that he always carried on his belt. It turned out that he had absently begun stropping the knife on the back of one of the coach seats, and the woman occupying the seat had become hysterical. "Get on your horse," Leo told him impatiently. "We're gettin' away from here!"

They hurried back to the express car where Leo, for the benefit of the train crew, tied up the agent. "Tell Mr. Blinn that we'll meet him where we said," the outlaw told him, "and divide up the money."

Agent Ford grinned. "I'll tell him."

"Well, so long, Mr. Ford," the outlaw said politely. "It's been right enjoyable doin' business with you. Maybe we'll meet up again sometime."

The expressman smiled brightly. "Not if I can help it," he said, but not before the outlaw was well out of hearing.

The trainmen stood beside the caboose looking stunned as the outlaws put their horses up the steep embankment, dragging the heavy strongbox on a makeshift travois. At last the engineer took off his cap and thoroughly wiped his face with a blue bandana. "Gents," he said after an extended period of fierce thought, "I'm beginnin' to get a feelin'. It wouldn't come as no great surprise," he sighed, "if there was considerable hell to pay for this."

At what they considered a safe distance from the train, the outlaws pulled up in a gully to give the strongbox a closer inspection. Across the top of the box was stenciled the legend, FREE STATE FEED AND GRAIN COMPANY. "That's her, all right!" Leo said happily. "Shoot 'er open somebody. I'm anxious to get a look at what forty thousand dollars looks like."

Rafe Jackson drew his Navy Colt and took dead aim on the heavy lock. The big .45 bellowed and the lock disappeared in a great boiling cloud of red dust. The bunch moved quickly to the box but no one touched it. They were waiting for Leo. This was an important occasion for the outlaw leader. After many heartbreaking false starts the gang had finally completed a successful robbery; it was a big day for Leo Brannon.

The outlaw stepped forward proudly and said

with a wide grin, "All right, boys, we'll just have ourselves a little look in this box." He grasped the iron lid in both hands and pulled it open.

For several endless seconds no one made a sound. They stood curiously slumped, their mouths hanging slightly open, staring blankly into the empty box. They did not even register surprise; they had known disappointment too often before to be very surprised by it this time. What they felt most of all at that moment was profound discouragement.

John Coyotesong was the first to speak. He stared long and hard into the empty box, then he turned to the gang leader and muttered accusingly, "And thee wouldn't let me take the ring!"

"Boys," Leo said in real misery, "I just don't understand this. I don't understand it at all."

"There ain't all that much to understand," Babe told him bitterly. "Mr. Bertrand Blinn, that big muck-a-muck with the feed and grain company, has double-crossed us. He stole the forty thousand dollars that was supposed to be in this box. But nobody'll ever *know* he stole it, because everybody'll be dead sure that *we* did." He threw his arms wide in an extravagant display of disgust. "Boys, I'm beginnin' to be of a mind that we wasn't never cut out to be outlaws!"

In the distance they could hear the huffing of the Katy locomotive. It no longer sounded complacent and friendly; it sounded angry and impatient.

"Somebody got theirselves a pry pole and cleared the tracks," Rafe Jackson said brightly.

John Coyotesong, his mind still on that ring, muttered something under his breath.

Then, for a few minutes, they all thought about the obliging Mr. Bertrand Blinn—but that, they soon realized, was an exercise in extreme futility. They would never again lay eyes on Mr. Blinn—nor agent Jack Ford. On this point there was not the slightest doubt in any of their minds.

Babe Brannon still had his arms outspread in helpless anger. "There's goin' to be hell to pay when that train gets to the next station. The telegraph'll have the story all over the Territory. When that happens I don't want to be anywhere near them Katy tracks."

The others nodded their heads dully.

"It's times like this," Babe said wearily, "that makes a man sorry he ever left the farm." He glanced at the little Comanche and grinned fiercely. "What about you, John? You ever sorry you left the reservation?"

The Indian only shrugged. Quaker Indian agents, or bumbling outlaw leaders like Leo, they were all *pukutsi*, crazy, as far as he was concerned. But he preferred the uncertainty of riding with the Brannons to eating issue beef on the reservation.

Leo looked around at the faces of his dejected followers. "If anybody's got any likely notions, I'm of a mind to listen."

They only looked at him.

"Well," the leader sighed, "I don't much fancy headin' west. Too many settlers and roads and telegraphs. I don't much like the notion of strikin' north; the Cherokee Light Horse're too thick, and so are the U. S. deputies. We might head east to Arkansas, but there'd only be more deputies to plague us." He smiled wanly. "Looks like it's the Choctaw country for us, boys."

They agreed with little shrugs and grunts. The rugged hill country of the Choctaw Nation was the last refuge for hunted men—it was better than ten years in a federal prison, but nobody had ever accused a wet cave in the Sans Bois of being a prime example of easy living.

With a striking lack of enthusiasm they got back in their saddles and struck south.

CHAPTER THREE

The sun was still an hour high when the hunting party made camp on the bank of the North Canadian. It had been a quiet and rather pleasant trip so far; Beeler had even worked up a fair amount of admiration for the Conmys and Ben Sutter. They rode the rough trails—or sometimes no trail at all—for long stretches of time without complaint. Beeler was beginning to realize that they were not quite the tenderfeet that they had seemed at first glance.

Once Verna Conmy had smiled and said, "Hunting trips—some in much more dangerous country than this—are not uncommon to Warren and Ben." She went on at some length to describe African safaris that they had been on, game that they had killed, trophies that they had taken. She said, "On the wall of Warren's study in Chicago is the head of a magnificent buffalo; the great, curving horns measure five feet from base to tip."

Beeler heard this bit of information with a great deal of skepticism. She had smiled with just the least bit of smugness. "The African buffalo and the American buffalo are two different animals. Quite different."

"Yes ma'am," Beeler said agreeably. "I guess so."

They rode on for a while in comfortable silence. From time to time Conmy and Sutter would suddenly spur away from the main column to take a look at some strange rock formation, or curious tree, or maybe for no reason at all other than high spirits. Verna Conmy would regard them affectionately and smile.

Once Beeler asked, "Is Mr. Conmy and your brother in business in Chicago?"

The question seemed to surprise her. "You've never heard of the Conmy-Sutter Packing Company?"

There were a lot of meat packers in Chicago; Beeler confessed that Conmy-Sutter was one that he had never heard of. "Well," she told him, "I don't suppose it's so strange at that. It was a large company once, but that was years ago, when my father and my husband's father owned it. Sometimes I forget that the name was changed when the company was sold to one of the big packing combines."

Little by little, as the party entered the Creek Nation and left the Oklahoma country behind them, Beeler pieced together the story of the Conmys and the Sutters. The packing company had been the business of the fathers of Beeler's present employers. When those owners died the company was sold for a great deal of money. Apparently Warren and Ben, with no company to occupy themselves with, spent a good deal of time traveling as they pleased and satisfying each whim as it occurred to them. The life seemed to agree with them completely. If there was a worry or dissatisfaction in any of their heads, Beeler could not discover it.

When Beeler decided to make camp, Conmy and Sutter grandly declined to take part in the work. "What's that I hear?" Sutter asked, as Beeler helped Humphrey O'Toole set up the bulky coal-oil stove.

Beeler cocked his head, listening to the faint gobbling sounds in the distance. "Turkeys," he said, "settlin' down to roost."

Conmy and Sutter beamed. "Turkey for supper, Hump! Don't start cookin' until we get back." The two men grabbed their rifles and left the camp in a stifling cloud of dust.

"A wagon cook would have their scalps for a trick like that," Beeler said irritably. But O'Toole, despite the heavy layer of dust that settled in his pots and pans, apparently had no complaint to make. Beeler was beginning to think that Conmy and Sutter could blow the camp up with blasting powder, and the peg-legged handyman would not complain. He could not help finding something curious in that kind of devotion.

"Hump," Verna Conmy told him, as she patiently waited for Beeler and Duane Keating to set up her tent, "goes back to the beginning of the Conmy-Sutter Packing Company. He worked for one of the English ranchers in Texas, but after he lost his leg in a trail accident, the Englishman decided that he didn't have any use for a peg-legged butler. My father hired him, and he's been with the family ever since." She told it casually, as if having the family butler on a hunting party was the most natural thing imaginable.

Well, Beeler thought to himself, all things considered, he guessed that he could teach himself to get along with the butler. But he was beginning to have doubts about Keating.

The most obvious thing about Conmy's secretary was that he was in love with his boss's wife. Beeler did not find this so very surprising—Verna Conmy was a strikingly beautiful woman. As obvious as his infatuation was, it didn't seem to bother anyone—and Beeler didn't find this so surprising either. Somehow Keating wasn't the kind of man who would ever give much concern to a Conmy or a Sutter.

"What exactly," Beeler had asked once, "does a secretary do?"

Verna Conmy had smiled absently. "I suppose that depends on who the secretary is. Duane is clever in business matters. When there is no business to attend to . . ." She shrugged a little. "Then I suppose he does whatever Warren and Ben ask him to do."

It must be very comforting, Beeler thought, to be so sure of yourself that you could keep a young man like Duane Keating on the payroll, knowing that he was in love with your wife.

The sound of the first rifleshot drifted downstream on the still summer air. Humphrey O'Toole lifted his head and grinned. "Turkey for supper," he said.

Then the second rifle sounded, and Beeler thought unhappily, *two* turkeys. Two gobblers at thirty pounds each was a lot of food for a party of six. He did not like the idea of wasted game; besides that, he had promised the Indians that only food and predators would be shot on the hunt.

Even as that thought was in his mind, the rifles began firing again. The shots crowded one on top of the other until the river bottom seemed to tremble with the roar. Through it all Verna Conmy merely smiled in her absent way. Humphrey O'Toole grinned and rubbed his hands together expectantly—in his mind he was already dreaming of stuffings and sauces. Duane Keating stood very still and listened to the roar of the rifles, his face pale. He made no sound.

Beeler grabbed up his own rifle. "What do the fools think they're doin'!" For one wild moment the thought crossed his mind that they were in trouble; that they had been attacked and were fighting for their lives. But there was nothing desperate about that shooting—it was thoughtful, measured, deliberate. It was the unmistakable sound of slaughter.

O'Toole and Verna Conmy stared at Beeler in amazement as he suddenly wheeled and raced upstream, not taking the time to saddle one of the horses. Duane Keating merely looked at him with a tight little smile. A smile that suggested that Beeler still had many things to learn about his employers.

The firing continued with rolling monotony now as Beeler crashed angrily through the brush. There on a small knoll, overlooking a stand of cottonwoods, stood Conmy and Sutter, just as Beeler had seen them in his mind. They stood shoulder to shoulder like infantrymen on the firing line, their rifles raised and smoking. They were laughing.

"One hundred dollars you owe me!" Sutter shouted happily as a large gobbler fell like a rock out of the cottonwood.

Conmy grinned, took quick aim and fired. "Not any more!" he laughed as another big bird fell to the ground.

For a moment Beeler stood stunned and sickened by what he saw. Gunsmoke swirled like ground fog around the little knoll. The whole area looked like some grotesque battlefield. The ground was covered with the dark bodies of dead birds. Wounded birds flapped about crazily with broken wings; blood, bright and crimson, glistened on the brown grass. A few of the turkeys, stupid birds that they were, circled in panic a few feet above the ground, but most of them clung to the trees where they made dark, beautiful targets in the late afternoon.

Beeler heard himself hollering, "Stop it! Stop it!"

Conmy lowered his rifle and looked back at him with a happy grin. "I never saw anything like it, Beeler! They just sit there and let you shoot them! This is the way it must have been with the buffalo once."

And now, Beeler thought grimly, there are no buffalo!

He came forward, his muscles taut and aching. As Sutter was getting ready to fire still again into the blood-spattered trees, Beeler grabbed his rifle, twisted it savagely out of his hand, and flung it away. He was about to lash out with his fists when a cold, still voice called from the brush. "None of that, mister! None of that!"

When Beeler didn't lower his hands immediately, a rifle crashed and a bullet snatched away a bit of sod an inch from his heel. Humphrey O'Toole stumped out of the brush, the stock of the rifle pressed firmly, expertly, next to his hip. Just how he had reached the knoll so quietly and so fast on a peg leg, Beeler didn't know.

Beeler let his hands drop slowly. For a moment he didn't trust himself to speak. In the pit of his stomach was that small, hated knot of fear. At last when he did speak, dryly, harshly, it was to O'Toole. "You're the third member of this party that has aimed a rifle at me. The next time any of you take it in your head to do it, my advice is to go ahead and shoot. At me, not at the ground at my feet."

Ben Sutter laughed. "Four, Beeler, not three. Look on the other side of the clearing."

Beeler wheeled, and there was Duane Keating, looking disturbingly cool and businesslike, with one of Conmy's silver-mounted Marlins at his shoulder. Warren Conmy chuckled quietly, as if at some secret joke. "It's all right, Keating," he said easily. "Mr. Beeler's just a little upset, that's all. You weren't actually going to hit anyone, were you, Beeler?"

Beeler's mouth tasted of acid and anger, but he was too old a hand to argue with two ready rifles. With a good deal of effort, he reined in his temper. "I guess you think it's unreasonable," he said finally, "but I mean it about the guns. I don't like havin' them pointed at me. The next time it happens, be ready to shoot."

"Settle down," Sutter said with a wide smile. "Nobody'll point guns at you if you don't like it. We didn't know you were so touchy. I would have thought that a deputy United States marshal would get used to such things."

"I never got used to it," Beeler said coldly.

"Well, it's all over now," Conmy said pleasantly. "Over and forgotten." He gestured lazily toward the ground littered with dead and wounded birds. "Hump, take your pick of the gobblers and get it ready for supper. Keating, you'd better get back to camp; Verna will want you to help her with the tent." As if nothing at all had happened, Ben Sutter sauntered over and picked up his rifle.

"There's one more thing," Beeler told him.

They looked at him blankly. Obviously, none of them had any idea what he was thinking. "The dead turkeys and the wounded," Beeler said. "Just what do you aim to do with them?"

"Do with them?" Ben Sutter's smooth forehead wrinkled slightly.

"The Creeks would run us out of the Territory in a minute if they ever got wind of this slaughter. The birds will have to be buried, and buried deep."

For several seconds they continued to look at him with those blank expressions of disbelief. "Are you serious?" Conmy asked at last.

"I'm serious. We might not get out of the Territory alive if some of the young hotbloods find out about this."

At last Conmy shrugged indifferently. "Well, I suppose you know about these things. Keating, you get the spade from camp and help Beeler bury the turkeys."

"I didn't kill them," Beeler said with a sudden, fierce grin. "I don't aim to bury them." With a stiff little nod, he turned and walked back to camp.

Surprisingly, Sutter and Conmy took Beeler's rebellion in the spirit of frontier fun. With

Keating's help, they killed the wounded birds, added them to the mountain of dead ones, and at last they buried them all together in a deep hole near the river. While they were doing that, Humphrey O'Toole scalded, dressed, and cleaned a thirty-pound gobbler. Beeler watched in fascination as the butler made his stuffing of rice, dried apricots, spices, and brandy. After the bird had been stuffed, he loosened the skin over the broad breast and inserted black wafers of French truffles. He worked quickly and efficiently on a folding table, by firelight.

"Does he do this kind of thing often?" Beeler asked Verna Conmy.

Mrs. Conmy smiled. "Not often. But Humphrey always manages to do his job well, whatever the conditions."

"He's a dead shot with a rifle, on top of other things. But I guess you know that."

"Of course. So is Duane Keating. Warren and Ben wouldn't have anyone working for them who couldn't shoot." She was sitting queenlike but quite relaxed on a folding campstool, smiling absently into the fire. Surprisingly, Beeler found her easy to talk to. She seemed pleased and proud of the small, rich world which sheltered and protected and amused the Conmys and the Sutters. Unlike her husband and her brother, she didn't seem to mind talking about it.

O'Toole trussed the bird with cotton string,

brushed it with butter, and put it in the oven over a coal-oil burner. "It's going to taste of coal oil," he said unhappily, shaking his head. "But there's nothing I can do about that."

Verna Conmy laughed—it was a light, musical sound. Nothing that had happened that afternoon seemed to disturb her in the least. Being first a Sutter, then a Conmy, perhaps she was immune to such things as the senseless slaughter of game. She looked at Beeler and said unexpectedly, "I know he doesn't show it, but my husband has a great deal of respect for your talents, Mr. Beeler."

He blinked. "What kind of talents would that be?"

"Hunting," she said, idly studying her fingernails by firelight. "Hunting men. Warren had Duane ask about you in Oklahoma City; he was very favorably impressed with your record."

"My record?"

"The four men you've killed," she said pleasantly. "And the dozens of others that you've run down and arrested. It is the kind of thing that Warren and Ben admire in a man." She smiled and shrugged her shoulders, as if to say all men were children and must be indulged in their whims.

Beeler was on the point of saying that he had never considered killing a thing to admire, but then he had the curious feeling that she would not know what he was talking about. At last he said, "Mrs. Conmy, I'd like to ask a favor of you."

“Of course, what is it?”

“I know that what you say can have a great deal of influence on your husband and your brother. I’d like it if you told them—in a nice way, of course—that I won’t stand for any more senseless slaughter of game.”

She turned and looked up at him with round blue eyes. “All right,” she said, as if she were pacifying a restless child. “I’ll tell them. Is it really so important?”

“Yes, ma’am,” he told her. “You see, I need this job, but I can’t go on working for Mr. Conmy if that’s the way he’s goin’ to hunt.”

It was well past nightfall when Conmy and Sutter and Duane Keating returned to camp. They were sweaty and tired from digging but seemed to be in good spirits—at least Conmy and Sutter were. Beeler was dimly amused at the glint of jealousy in Keating’s eyes when he saw Beeler talking so casually to Mrs. Conmy.

The men washed up at the river and returned to the camp as O’Toole was taking the turkey out of the small oven. “It smells of coal oil,” the butler complained.

To Frank Beeler it smelled like Thanksgiving and Christmas and the Fourth of July rolled into one, only better. They ate at the small camp table, now set with white linen and old silver. Beeler had not known that such food existed. The aroma of black truffles perfumed the night air of the Creek

Nation—Beeler almost laughed when he thought about it. For the moment he could almost forgive Conmy and Sutter for the turkey slaughter. He could even forgive O'Toole for throwing down on him with a loaded rifle and shooting within an inch of his body. Almost.

They drank ruby-red burgundy from the vineyards of *Clos de Beze.* Afterward the men smoked delicately dappled cigars from Cuba and drank brandy that was already rich and mature when Napoleon was being exiled to Elba. Beeler concentrated on enjoying it all to its fullest, for he was sure that he would never savor its likes again.

Through the comfortable sense of well-being that followed the meal, Beeler slowly became aware of Conroy and Sutter looking at him. Conmy smiled brightly, heaved a huge sigh of satisfaction, and said, "Well, Beeler?"

Beeler spread his hands on the linen cloth. "I never had a supper like it before, and that's the truth."

"I'm glad that you enjoy the good things of life," Conmy smiled.

"Hard luck for me. Most good things come expensive."

Conmy and Sutter looked at one another and laughed. Sutter blew a cloud of smoke toward the summer sky. "We are prepared to pay you five hundred dollars for a few days' work. There are many good things in life available for much less."

For several seconds Beeler merely grinned at the night. *Five hundred dollars.* In that hard time year of 1890, it was a sum to take a man's breath away.

Conmy said quietly, "What do you say, Beeler?"

Beeler lowered his cigar and looked at them. They were waiting quietly, tensely, for his reply.

For a while Beeler did not know what to say. A short time ago, when he broke up the turkey slaughter, he had expected to be fired on the spot—instead of firing him they had fed him a supper such as he had never tasted before, and now, incredibly, they were offering him five hundred dollars.

"The job shouldn't take more than a week," Ben Sutter said. "Anything over a week we'd pay extra."

Beeler's head was beginning to swim. They were all watching him with blank faces. Smiling blank smiles. Even O'Toole, who was washing dishes on the other side of the tent, was now standing like a peg-legged statue, waiting to see what Beeler's response would be.

"What would I be expected to do," Beeler asked at last, "to earn so much money in such a short time?"

All of them seemed to breathe little sighs of relief. Conmy leaned forward, his elbows on the table. "We're after a different kind of game on this hunt," he said slowly. "Ben and I are not familiar with the country, so we need you to guide us. That's all there is to it."

A warning ripple went up Beeler's back. "In Oklahoma City, you said you were after wolves."

"That's right. We are. Human wolves."

It took Beeler a few seconds to digest the meaning of those two words. "Outlaws," he said at last. "Men. You want me to guide you on a hunt to kill men."

"The only game really worth hunting," Conmy said quickly. "You ought to know that better than anyone, Beeler."

"I never killed men for sport."

Ben Sutter leaned forward suddenly. "Are you sure, Beeler? Think back on it. Are you sure there wasn't the taste of excitement in your mouth as you tracked your man down and finally got him in your sights. Think. Wasn't there a big, swelling sense of satisfaction and accomplishment in your chest, almost bursting, when you squeezed the trigger and brought him down?"

Beeler stared at them. He wasn't angry, because he couldn't completely believe what was happening. Everybody but Verna Conmy was watching him intently—Verna's interest had waned and she was now gazing idly into the campfire. Probably thinking up a menu for the next day, Beeler thought grimly, to talk over with O'Toole.

"Five hundred dollars," Duane Keating spoke for the first time. "You were more than willing to be our guide for a mere three dollars a day. Think of what you could do with five hundred!"

"Five hundred dollars," Beeler told them dryly, "would solve just about every problem I've got. But I don't think I want to commit murder for it."

"Murder!" Warren Conmy appeared to be shocked by the very thought. "Nobody said anything about murder. Nobody's suggesting that you do anything illegal or immoral. In those hills of the Choctaw Nation there are outlaws—you said so yourself—murderers, robbers, rapists, the very scum of the human race. They're all wanted by the law; dead or alive, most of them. A great many of them, I imagine, have prices on their heads." He smiled quickly. "Any such bounty would belong entirely to you, of course. Ben and I would not put in a claim."

Beeler said stiffly. "No."

Because he made no violent argument against the scheme, Conmy and Sutter assumed that he was fishing for more money. Ben Sutter said, "We might raise your guarantee to six hundred. Or even seven, in the case of a satisfactory hunt."

As a matter of real curiosity, Beeler asked, "What would you consider satisfactory?"

"There must be at least two . . ." He searched his mind for the right word. "Two trophies. Wanted outlaws, with prices on their heads." His smile was just the least bit sheepish. "You see, that's the only way of knowing who the winner is."

Beeler stared at them in amazement. When he had ridden for the Fort Smith court he had got to know his share of killers, but he could not recall any as casually cold-blooded as the ones before him now. He said to Ben, “You and Mr. Conmy have a bet. Is that it?”

Ben Sutter shrugged. “Well, sort of.”

“The one that kills the outlaw with the biggest price on his head is the winner?”

Verna Conmy drew in her vacant gaze and rejoined the discussion for a moment. “I told you they were like children,” she smiled.

Children who caught rabbits in steel traps and then turned them loose with their legs broken. Beeler had known children like that.

Duane Keating spoke again, sounding exasperated with Beeler for the unreasonable stand he had taken. “I don’t understand why you hesitate to take the job; it’s the same job you were doing when you were a deputy marshal.”

“I was working for the law then.”

Conmy heaved a loud sigh and appeared to be taking the whole thing philosophically. “Perhaps you’ll think about it. Let us know tomorrow, or the next day.”

Beeler shook his head. “There’s nothin’ to think about. You’ll just have to get yourself another guide.”

They sat for a while in silence. The night was warm and soft—like a pretty woman, Beeler thought wryly. For a moment the vision of Elizabeth Stans was in his mind—but somehow the vision was not quite as pretty as it once had been. The unavoidable comparison with Verna Conmy—Beeler was forced to admit—did not do Elizabeth any good.

"I think," Warren Conmy said at last, "the best thing under the circumstances is to get a good night's rest. Mr. Sutter and I will have to cancel our wager, and tomorrow we'll continue the hunt as first planned." He smiled brilliantly to assure Beeler that there were no hard feelings.

Beeler was not assured. But neither was he eager to quit a good job, if it could be saved. "Whatever you say. Tomorrow we'll strike south toward the Sans Bois."

CHAPTER FOUR

The outlaws were in the Choctaw Nation, somewhere north of the old stage station of Perryville, when they first encountered the posse. Rafe Jackson, scouting ahead of the others, drew first fire.

Leo Brannon listened to the angry spatter of rifle fire with a look of profound depression. He had been hoping to make it to the hill country before a posse located them—but that was a great deal to hope for in this modern age of railroads and telegraphs. Babe Brannon and John Coyotesong looked at Leo, waiting for instructions. That was the trouble with being the leader, somebody was always waiting for you to tell them what to do.

"Boys," Leo told them unhappily, "it looks like we're goin' to have to scrap our way out of this."

In a few minutes Rafe Jackson came fogging it out of the wooded draw. "Posse!" Rafe told them excitedly. "Mad as yellow jackets in a brush fire, but can't shoot worth a damn. Way I figger it, there's maybe one deputy marshal and four or five white intruders that he's hired as possemen."

That made Leo feel a little better. Dollar-a-day possemen weren't famous for taking long chances. "Over there . . ." Rafe pointed. "There's a pretty good stand of timber; I figger that's the best place to make our play."

The outlaws reached the high ground a few minutes ahead of the posse. One of the possemen flew through the air like a circus trapeze artist when Babe downed his horse with a lucky rifleshot.

But the possemen didn't know it was luck. They pulled up sharply and began scattering in all directions on the exposed slope.

The outlaws threw themselves down in the brush and peppered the undignified retreat with rifle fire. To Leo Brannon, it was all pretty discouraging. "Boys," he said wearily to no one in particular, "I've just about concluded that one reason we've done so poorly in the train robbin' business is that nobody amongst us, except maybe John, can shoot worth a damn."

For several minutes they lay taking casual shots at the brush at the bottom of the slope. At last Babe said in disgust, "All we're doin' is shootin' up our shells. I say we ought to light out of here, the quicker the better."

"Horses tired," John Coyotesong said laconically.

"Well, maybe the posse's horses are tired too."

After some agonizingly painful thought, Leo Brannon told them, "I figger we'll just stay where we are a spell. Wait and see what happens." That was Leo's response to any crisis. Wait and see. And hope for the best.

So, burrowed in the heavy brush of wild-plum thicket, they waited. What action they could see at the bottom of the slope seemed to be confused and undirected. Hired possemen made poor help, as that deputy marshal was obviously learning. But at least they were armed, and any man with a gun in his hand was dangerous, as the Brannon bunch had plenty of reason to know.

They had been in their position for the best part of an hour, when Leo suddenly looked around and said, "Where's John?"

Rafe Jackson, who had been on the verge of dozing off, roused himself and blinked his watery eyes. "He was here just a little while ago."

They all sat up and looked around wonderingly, but they did not see the little Comanche. There was a slight depression in the grass, a little to the left where Rafe had been lying, but John Coyotesong was not there. "Boys," Leo Brannon said nervously, "you don't reckon old John decided to throw in with the law, do you?"

Babe snorted. The sight of a Comanche throwing in with a bunch of lawmen was more than he could imagine. On the other hand, of course, a lot of people couldn't imagine a Quahada Comanche throwing in with *any* bunch of white men, even outlaws.

Another half-hour passed and still there was no sign of John Coyotesong. Not a shot had been fired for almost twenty minutes. "What do you reckon they're doin' down there anyhow?" Leo wondered out loud.

"If I was them," Babe said, with a touch of acid in his tone, "I'd do just what they're doin'. Station four or five men around this knoll and try to hold us where we are . . . and send one man for help."

Leo was alarmed. "You reckon they'd really do a thing like that?"

"I almost forgot," Rafe Jackson said brightly. "I seen one of their boys ridin' off to the north as I was comin' up the grade."

The leader of the bunch groaned helplessly. Against his every natural instinct, he knew that he had to make a decision. Babe and Rafe were not much comforted as they watched their leader try to settle on one of several disasters that lay ahead of them. Then, at the last minute, he was saved by a sudden burst of pistol fire from the bottom of the slope.

"Damnation!" Leo said in a startled tone. "What're they up to now?"

All together there were five shots, followed by an outburst of high-pitched whooping and hollering. "That's John!" Rafe Jackson said. "What the hell's he think he's doin'?"

Babe Brannon began to grin. Following John's series of scalp-tingling war whoops, they heard the pound of hooves. "That damn Comanche's runnin' off their horses!" he said happily.

The outlaws hurried to the far side of their wooded knoll, and sure enough, there was John Coyotesong scrambling for his life up the grassy slope. His friends directed their rifles at the bottom of the slope and fired steadily. But there was very little shooting in return. Apparently the amateur possemen had been thrown into confusion, if not panic, by the loss of their horses. They could hear the deputy marshal hollering angrily for them to forget the animals and keep their attention on the outlaws at the top of the knoll. But by that time it was too late.

"Thee get my horse," the little Indian panted to Rafe Jackson. "We better go now." He sat on the ground to get his breath. With a calm that amounted almost to indifference, he watched the wild scurrying below. In their day the Quahadas had been the best horse thieves of all the Plains tribes; he couldn't get very excited about running off a few horses of dollar-a-day possemen.

Around midafternoon that day, Frank Beeler directed the fording of the South Canadian and led his party into the Choctaw Nation. There had been no more talk of the macabre hunt for outlaws. Apparently Sutter and Conmy had put the thought out of their minds and had contented themselves with a regular hunt for regular game.

"Over there's where you'll find your wolves." Beeler pointed to the east, toward a darkly wooded ridge of hills "Timber wolves. Big ones, and plenty of them. They'll make good trophies for you."

Conmy and Sutter smiled and nodded. If their minds seemed to be on something else, Beeler put it down to the long day in the saddle.

It was almost time to make camp when the lone horsebacker topped a distant rise and waved to them excitedly. He hollered something, but they couldn't make out what it was. Conmy and Sutter turned to their scout with raised eyebrows.

"We better wave him in and see what's the matter," Beeler told them reluctantly. He somehow had the feeling that life would have been more peaceful if that horseman had not crossed their trail.

"I'm sure enough glad to see you folks," the rider said breathlessly, as he reined up at the head of the column. "There's hell to pay over there in the valley. A deputy marshal and five possemen have got the Brannon bunch trapped on top of a timbered rise, but they need help to bring them in." For a moment he admired the silver-mounted rifles that Conmy and Sutter carried in their saddle boots. "If you folks wouldn't mind comin' along and givin' a hand, I'd be much obliged. And so would the marshal."

"The Brannon bunch!" Conmy said, his eyes bright and lively. "Aren't they the train robbers?"

"That's the bunch. Killed I don't know how many men. Robs nigh every train that comes through the Territory. They're hellers, all right. But the marshal figgers he can bring them in if he gets some help."

Conmy grinned at Beeler. “What about it, Beeler? Don’t you think we ought to help the marshal out?”

Conmy and Sutter looked at each other, and Beeler saw the happy glint in their eyes. The bet was on again. The hunt would be for human wolves, after all.

But Beeler shook his head to the posseman. “I’m sorry, but this is a huntin’ party. I’m the guide and I couldn’t allow them to go up against a bunch like the Brannons. Besides, we’ve got a lady with the party.”

The posseman did not look particularly surprised. He could understand how a person might not be eager to face up to an outlaw gang like the Brannons. He shrugged resignedly. “Well, no harm in askin’. I’ll go on to Perryville and get somebody there.”

“Just a minute,” Ben Sutter said quickly. “Keating and O’Toole can stay behind with Verna and make camp. Verna won’t mind.”

Verna Conmy gave her brother an indulgent smile.

“I think we ought to do it,” Conmy put in before Beeler could object. “It seems to me it’s our duty. Of course, the decision is up to Mr. Beeler,” he told the posseman. “He’s the guide.”

But Sutter was not ready to let it rest quite yet. “As a former deputy marshal yourself, Beeler, I should think you’d be eager to give the lawman a hand.”

Now the posseman did look surprised. He looked Beeler over carefully, as if trying to decide what kind of man he was to let a fellow lawman's request for help go unheeded. The look bordered on contempt, and it bothered Beeler more than he liked to admit.

The posseman scowled. "Is that right, mister? Was you one time a deputy marshal?"

Beeler shrugged, realizing that he couldn't just sit there and let the lawman stew in his own sweat. "All right," he sighed, "I guess you better show us where the trouble's at."

Marshal Sid Gifford sat on a fallen cottonwood with his rifle across his knees and a profound look of disgust on his face. When he heard his posseman returning with the three horsebackers, he didn't even bother to look around. Within the past hour he had lost in the neighborhood of two thousand dollars in bounty and maybe much more. When he thought of how long it would take him to earn that much riding for the federal court it made him want to take something in his two big hands—preferably a posseman—and do it violence.

"Marshal?" Frank Beeler leaned over his horse's neck and looked down at him. "Are you all right?"

Gifford, his face set like stone, looked up at Beeler. "What do you want?"

"Your posseman crossed our trail a while back

and said you might be needin' help. Is there anything we can do?"

"There ain't nothin' nobody can do," the lawman said grimly. "A while back you could of saved me two thousand dollars. But not any more. It's gone with the Brannons."

"Was it really the Brannons you had trapped here?"

"Trapped." The marshal grinned bitterly. "Oh, they were the Brannons all right. I been followin' them for the best part of two days. They robbed the Katy up in the Creek Nation and got forty thousand dollars in a strongbox."

Beeler whistled softly. Now he understood how the marshal had lost two thousand dollars; somebody had put a bounty on the outlaws' heads. After a moment Beeler asked, "Do you want to tell us what happened?"

The marshal threw his arms wide and heaved a huge sigh. With a good deal of hostility he looked at Warren Conmy and Ben Sutter. A pair of dudes. Silver-mounted rifles on their saddles. Well, he consoled himself, probably it didn't matter that help was an hour too late in coming. He couldn't imagine how a pair of city boys could have been much help against the Brannons. "One of the outlaw bunch," he said, "sneaked down from that knoll up there and ran off our horses. That's what happened." He forced a small grin. "Well, that's what comes of hirin' your own possemen. To cap it off, the court probably won't accept more'n half of what I claim in expenses, and I'll have to pay them out of my own pocket."

Beeler smiled. He knew the problem well.

Far down the draw, at the base of the knoll, they could hear the possemen thrashing around, still looking for their animals. Conmy said eagerly, "We've got three horses now, not counting the one your posseman's on. Couldn't we go after them?"

Gifford shook his head dejectedly. "No use. They're halfway to the Sans Bois by this time. Anyhow, it'll be dark in another half-hour. No . . ." He shook his head some more. "I'll just wait till tomorrow and hope to pick up their trail again."

"And if you don't?"

The marshal shrugged. "Somebody else will. There's a thousand-dollar bounty on Leo Brannon's head and five hundred on the others."

Conmy and Sutter seemed to find this talk of bounty distasteful. "I was under the impression," Ben Sutter said, "that it was unethical for a peace officer to accept bounty money."

Gifford looked startled at such a suggestion. "I don't know about unethical, mister, but if the lawman ain't crazy in the head he takes his bounty whenever he can get it." He grinned crookedly at Beeler. "Thanks anyhow, but there ain't anything you can do now. You might as well get back to your huntin' party."

Conmy and Sutter were bitterly disappointed.

As they were riding back to camp, Conmy asked, "Do you think the outlaws will make for the hill country, like the marshal said?"

Beeler shrugged. "The Sans Bois, most likely. That's where I would head, if I was them."

"What if we run into them?"

"We won't."

"How can you be so sure?"

"Leo Brannon knows those hills. He wouldn't hole up any place a huntin' party would ever see."

Almost as if he could see the thought in Beeler's mind, Ben Sutter smiled and said gently, "One thousand dollars on Leo Brannon's head alone. A lot of money, Beeler. It could all be yours."

Beeler looked at him but did not answer. He told himself that such a proposition did not deserve an answer. Was that it? Or was he simply afraid to say anything at all, for fear that he would find himself agreeing to do what they wanted?

It was well past dark when they reached camp where O'Toole's campfire and coal-oil stove made a cheery light in the night. "I didn't know how long you'd be," the butler told Conmy. "Will omelets be all right?"

"Omelets will do," Conmy told him, not bothering to disguise the bitter disappointment in his voice.

Beeler lit a cigar and walked over to where Duane Keating was tightening a rope of Mrs. Conmy's tent. "I take it," the secretary said dryly, "the expedition was not a success."

"Nobody got killed, if that's what you mean."

Keating thought about this for a moment. He seemed vaguely pleased. "The outlaws got away?"

"They were gone when we got there."

"What will you do now?"

"Go on with the hunt, the way we planned in Oklahoma City." Beeler sat on a folding camp-stool and studied Keating for some time. "How long," he asked at last, "have you been with the Conmys?"

"Almost four years. We've known each other much longer, of course."

"You have?"

Keating smiled in a strange way. "We were children together in Chicago. I supposed that someone had told you."

"Told me what?"

"My father was the one who started the Conmy-Sutter Packing Company. Warren's and Ben's fathers worked for him . . . in the beginning."

Beeler was getting interested. "What happened?"

"My father made some . . . unwise investments and lost the company." He smiled that smile again. "I believe Humphrey has supper on the table now."

Beeler kept his seat for a few more minutes while the others got ready to eat. Well, well, he thought to himself. First it had been the *Keating*

Packing Company. Then old Sutter and Conmy had somehow done him out of it, and then it was the Conmy-Sutter Company. And now young Keating was Warren Conmy's personal secretary and, incidentally, in love with his boss's wife. All of which was very interesting, but, he reminded himself, none of Frank Beeler's business.

He brought his folding stool to the table and sat with the others. "Tomorrow," he said, helping himself to O'Toole's omelet, "we'll make the Sans Bois foothills. Won't find much in the way of trails, but there's plenty of game."

Conmy and Sutter bent over their plates and ate in silence. Keating was formally attentive to Verna Conmy, but his mind seemed to be on other things. Mrs. Conmy chatted idly to no one in particular, but didn't seem to have her heart in it.

Beeler began to be uncomfortably aware of the coolness of his employers. On the surface they were civil and not unpleasant, but he could feel that the party had gone sour.

It was early the next morning that Babe Brannon's horse pulled up lame. They were somewhere south of Brushy Creek, barely into the foothills of the Sans Bois Mountains.

Thanks to John Coyotesong, they had escaped the deputy marshal and his possemen, but during the night Rafe Jackson had seen a firelight flickering far to the north as he was standing guard.

Campfire. It could mean anything. Maybe it was a family of Indians; during the summer they were always traveling from place to place to visit kinfolks and friends. Maybe it was the marshal still looking for his horse. Or—as they feared most—a new posse of professional lawmen.

In any event, the horse was done for as a saddle animal. Between muttered curses and groans, Babe stripped it and turned it loose. "We'll just have to take turns walkin' and ridin'," Leo sighed. He pointed to a high ridge capped with sandstone. "Up there's where we'll make for. There's caves in them rocks where not even a coon dog could sniff us out. Rafe, you lay behind and keep an eye on our backtrail."

Rafe tied his horse, found himself a rock ledge to sit on, and prepared to wait. It was midmorning when he first saw the pack train crawling over the brown prairie, making for the hills. What kind of an outfit it was he didn't know, but it didn't take him long to decide that he didn't like the looks of it. At midday he chewed some jerky and drank some water from his canteen and moved on up into the hills. The pack train kept coming. Rafe waited until there was no doubt about where it was headed, then he got his horse and made for the sandstone cap where the bunch was waiting.

"Indians," Leo said when Rafe told him what he had seen.

Rafe shook his head. "They wasn't Indians."

“Maybe a railroad surveyin’ outfit.”

“There’s a woman with them.”

Leo groaned impatiently. “Why didn’t you say so! It’s some kind of fancy huntin’ party; most likely a bunch of dudes from back East. They won’t come this far into the hills.”

“What if they do?”

“I told you, they won’t. Put it out of your mind and help John rustle some firewood.”

Babe Brannon sat on a flat rock in front of the cave, nursing his blistered feet. It had been a hard climb up from the foothills, and he had done most of it on foot. “I wonder,” he said to his brother, “how you can be so damn sure that huntin’ party ain’t nothin’ to worry about?”

“Because,” Leo told him loftily, “I’ve seen dudes before and I know they ain’t goin’ to scratch up their fancy clothes climbin’ these hills.”

But that night he sent John Coyotesong backtracking to take another look. John came back and reported seeing another campfire and what might have been two or three tents. “There you are,” Leo said with satisfaction. “A bunch of dudes.”

“Maybe,” Babe grunted, “but dudes ain’t blind. If they cross our trail and report it to another bunch of possemen . . .” He let that unpleasant thought dangle for a while. The glum outlaws sat around their own small fire, chewing their emergency rations of jerky and drinking coffee made from leftover grounds. “Boys,” Babe said at last,

"I don't like to say it, the shape my feet's in, but tomorrow we better do some more climbin'."

They climbed all the next day, clawing their way through the wild tangle of scrub brush and rock. This was true outlaw country now, pitted with caves, laced with deer trails that had the unnerving habit of dead-ending without warning and becoming deathtraps. When nightfall came, Leo Brannon fell to the ground and gasped triumphantly, "Boys, we're as safe now as your old grandpappy in his rockin' chair back home. That bunch of dudes, or nobody else, ain't *never* goin' to find us here!"

At that moment, as Leo reassured his fellow outlaws, Warren Conmy was gazing up at those rugged ridges with a curious smile. "Hump," he told the family butler, "no fires tonight. Not even in the stove. We'll eat something cold, whatever you've got in cans."

He and Ben Sutter walked off a short distance from camp and stood in the gathering dusk, staring in fascination at the hills while bullbats swooped and cut wide circles in the air over their heads. At last Beeler walked up to them and said, "You might as well put it out of your minds. We're not goin' after the Brannons."

"Nobody said we were," Sutter smiled.

"But that's what you've been thinkin' ever since we spotted that lamed pony today. There's no way of knowin' it belonged to one of the outlaws."

"But it could have," Conmy said gently. "It makes an interesting theory. The outlaw bunch up there somewhere, one of them afoot. That would hinder their movement considerably, wouldn't you think?"

"I don't think about it," Beeler told him. "You shouldn't, either. I'm not goin' to take you huntin' outlaws."

Conmy and Sutter smiled quietly. "We know," Conmy said mildly. "We're not asking you to do anything against your principles."

Beeler was not satisfied, but he decided not to make an issue of it. For supper they ate canned tomatoes and beans and hard bread spread with liver paste. There was no fire. It was out of concern for his wife, Conmy explained, that he did not want to attract possible trouble by showing a light to the outlaws. "Tomorrow," he told Beeler, "I think we'll double back and make for Brushy Creek again. That would be the safest thing all around, don't you think?"

That was exactly what Beeler thought, but it wasn't like Conmy and Sutter to be brought around so easily.

As he went with O'Toole to water the horses and put them out to graze, he could hear Sutter and the Conmys chattering animatedly in front of Verna Conmy's tent. They sounded completely happy and carefree, which he reasoned, was exactly as it should be. They were young people on an outing. *Rich* young people. Under such circumstances, it ought to be easy to be happy and carefree.

For a while he made an effort to think about Elizabeth Stans. But Elizabeth was far away; and in the back of his mind he kept hearing the happy laughter and talk of the Conmys and Ben Sutter. Why was it that such a happy sound put a chill in his guts?

It was still dark when Beeler rolled out of his blankets the next morning. The day was soft and pleasant and glistening with dew. A good day, he thought. Soon they would be out of this particular part of the Sans Bois and go on with the hunt.

He didn't believe a word of it. He wasn't sure why, but he didn't believe it.

O'Toole was already up. Together they went to the stream and washed. When they got back to camp the hills were shining coldly in the early dawn. Keating had the fire going and had started coffee. Verna Conmy stepped outside her tent, looking fresh and beautiful. It looked like the beginning of a perfect day, Beeler thought to himself. Except for one thing. Warren Conmy and Ben Sutter were not there.

Verna looked at him in wide amusement when he asked about them. "Mr. Beeler," she chided, "you ought to know by this time how they are together. Like children. Impulsive."

"Did they take it in their heads," Beeler said

coldly, "to go after the Brannon bunch by theirselves?"

She smiled absently. "I really can't say. Warren and Ben rarely reveal their plans to anyone."

"When did they pull out?"

"Sometime during the night. I'm not sure."

Beeler wheeled and called to Keating. "Bring up two horses and get your rifle!" To Verna he snapped, "Do you always allow them to do whatever enters their heads? Don't you ever try to stop them?"

The question seemed to startle her. "Of course not. Why should I?"

CHAPTER FIVE

Rafe Jackson was making his usual early morning scout of their backtrail when the bullet knocked him down. He had been standing on a tall outcrop, admiring the shimmering dawn and thinking absently about Arkansas, which was just beyond the fartherest ridge of hills and was his home, when the .30-caliber tin-and-lead slug tore without warning through the soft part of his throat.

Rafe never knew what hit him. He never heard the rifle that fired the shot that killed him. He simply stared for an instant, stunned and shocked, as the life went out of him. Then he fell forward, down the side of the outcrop and landed face down in the dirt.

Rafe Jackson, family man and sometime farmer, when conditions allowed, part-time outlaw and train robber, when they didn't, was dead.

From the far side of a narrow gorge Ben Sutter whooped with delight. Grinning widely, he jerked off his hat and waved it to Warren Conmy who had watched the shot from some hundred yards down the rocky slope. Warren waved back and grinned ruefully. Ben, as usual, had drawn first blood.

The two men scrambled up the rocky incline to inspect their kill. For several minutes they stood looking down at Rafe Jackson's still figure. "For an outlaw," Sutter said at last, "he sure doesn't look like much." He sounded disappointed, as if he had gone to a good deal of trouble to shoot a giant elk only to discover that the antlers were damaged. "Wonder which one he is?"

"Look in his pockets, maybe there's something to tell us."

They got down on their knees, rolled Rafe over as if he were a side of meat and methodically began going through his pockets. "One pocketknife," Conmy said, checking the items off one by one. "A stub pencil, three .45-caliber cartridges, a half dollar, a nickel-plated watch." He held the watch to his ear for a moment. "It's not running. Ben, doesn't it seem to you that one of the Brannon outlaws ought to have more than half a dollar in his pocket? According to that posseman, the bunch took forty thousand dollars in one holdup alone."

Sutter shrugged. "Probably they've got the money at their main camp, wherever that is."

"Wait a minute," Conmy said, digging into Rafe's shirt pocket. "Here's something." He drew out a sack of tobacco, almost empty, a few wheatstraw papers, and a battered letter. As it had been Sutter's kill, Conmy handed him the letter.

Slowly, and with a good deal of difficulty, Ben read the childish scrawl. "The man's name is Rafe Jackson," he said finally. "The letter's from his wife in Arkansas telling him that his son is dead of something called the 'summer complaint.' "

Conmy looked surprised. "I didn't know outlaws had families."

"This one did." Sutter folded the letter and put it back in the dead man's pocket. "Well," he sighed, "anyway we know that he's not Leo Brannon, the leader. You've still got a chance of winning the bet."

Beeler and Keating were two hours out of camp when they heard the flat, insignificant report of a single rifle. The secretary cocked his head slightly and smiled at Beeler. "We're too late. They've already found the outlaws. One of them, anyway."

"How do you know the outlaws didn't find them?"

"I know the way Ben and Warren shoot. I've never known them to miss the game they went after, no matter what it was."

Angrily, Beeler tugged his hat down on his forehead and put his dun gelding up the rocky deer path. "Up there"—he pointed to a white sandstone outcrop—"is where the shot came from."

"We're wearing our horses out for nothing," Keating told him with a shrug. "When we get there we'll only find a dead man, and it won't be Ben or Warren."

Keating was partly right. When they got to the place there was a dead man. There was also

Conmy and Sutter, casually smoking cigars while they inspected the dead man's effects. For several long seconds Beeler merely stared at them. He had watched men hang on the monstrous twelve-man gallows at Fort Smith who had not been half as cold-blooded as this pair.

Beeler heard himself saying in a strangely thin voice, "What the hell do you think you're doin'?"

Conmy looked at him blankly. "Ben just killed an outlaw, that's all."

"How do you know he's an outlaw?"

"His name is Rafe Jackson, one of the Brannon outlaws. There's a letter in his pocket to prove it."

"But you didn't know that when you shot him, did you?"

For the first time Conmy and Sutter detected some of the cold fury behind Beeler's words. Their eyes became cautious. It was Conmy who spoke. "Beeler, this is none of your business. Get back to camp, move everything back a few miles from these hills, and make sure that my wife is safe. That's what we're paying you for now."

"Sutter has murdered a man. Do you expect me to just ride off and make like it never happened?"

"Ben killed an outlaw with a price on his head. I wouldn't call that murder."

"Warren and I don't expect to collect the bounty, of course," Ben Sutter said pleasantly. "It can be yours, Beeler. All you have to do is put in the claim. Five hundred dollars, I believe the posseman said—all for doing nothing but keeping your mouth shut."

Keating saw the little spots of anger in Beeler's cheeks and smiled to himself. With a deliberateness that was unmistakably threatening, the former marshal got down from his dun. Warren Conmy's eyes widened just a little; he raised his rifle and casually aimed it at Beeler's middle. "We're offering you a good thing, Beeler. Don't do something foolish and ruin it for yourself."

But Beeler was not listening. His entire attention now was on the rifle in Conmy's hands. Still, Conmy was not greatly disturbed. It did not occur to him that Beeler might attack him while looking into the muzzle of a loaded rifle.

It was a serious mistake on Conmy's part. He watched for an instant, fascinated, as a bird might watch the weaving head of a snake, as Beeler simply reached out and moved the rifle barrel to one side. Almost immediately a rock-hard fist loomed in Conmy's face and exploded.

Conmy reeled back, wildly flinging his arms about in an effort to break his fall. He fell to his hands and knees, his eyes glazed, his face bloody.

"I told you," Beeler said in a voice that shook, "never to point a gun at me unless you meant to shoot."

He took a step forward. He would have struck Conmy again if Sutter hadn't spoken. "I believe you meant that warning for both of us," he said coolly. "Well, it's my turn now, Beeler. And I don't mind shooting."

Sutter had brought his rifle to his shoulder and was aiming carefully at Beeler's heart. Like an expert marksman intent on the exact center of his target, he quietly began squeezing the trigger.

"Ben, wait!" Conmy lurched to his feet, with blood welling up at the corner of his mouth and dripping off the point of his chin.

"Why wait?" Ben asked. "We can kill him and bury him in the rocks and no one will ever know."

"No, we need him. Beeler knows these hills; we don't. We need a guide to lead us to the other outlaws. What about it, Beeler?"

To Beeler's amazement, Conmy even managed a bloody smile. "You see, Beeler," Conmy went on, dabbing at his mouth, "I understand your reluctance to conduct the kind of hunt we ask for—but think of the benefits to yourself if you do it. The five hundred dollars, for one thing, as well as any other bounty that Ben and I might earn. Also, there's the even more basic matter of staying alive. Ben can kill you in an instant—and he will, unless you come quickly to the right decision."

Beeler glanced quickly at Sutter and knew that he would not hesitate to kill him, just as he had not hesitated to kill Rafe Jackson. To Conmy, he said, "Is this pastime of murdering outlaws so important to you?"

"Anything I make up my mind to do is important to me. And I've made up my mind to hunt the Brannon bunch down and kill them. It's a matter of pride with Ben and me, you understand."

"Mister," Beeler told him truthfully, "I don't understand anything about you, or your brother-in-law, or any of your outfit. As for the Brannons, maybe they need killin'—I don't know that much about them. But I don't aim to lead you on a hunt so you can shoot them down for sport, like they was a pack of wolves."

Conmy shrugged. "Are you deliberately asking Ben to shoot you?"

"I'm askin' to be cut free of this whole fandango. I don't even want any pay. Go back to Perryville and hire yourself another guide; maybe you can find somebody that'll do the kind of job you want."

Conmy was holding a white linen handkerchief to his mouth. He shook his head sadly from side to side. "We can't do it, Beeler. If you went back and told your story the way you seem to understand it . . . well, there might be some people who wouldn't understand our side. It could mean bad publicity for the family. It could make it awkward for us when we got back to Chicago."

Beeler felt a cold breath on the back of his neck. Until this instant he had figured that if he could live through the first few seconds he would have a good chance of getting away alive. Now he wasn't at all sure that he would be allowed to go on living, no matter which way he turned. He could see the still coolness in Sutter's eyes. Ben was tired of waiting; he wanted to get it over with.

"You'd go ahead and kill me," Beeler asked in a voice that was slightly dazed, "just because I might make things awkward for you in Chicago?"

Conmy smiled. "That's about it."

It was becoming clearer by the second that they were giving him up as a bad bargain. Even Keating, observing the drama from his saddle, had obviously marked Beeler down as dead.

Beeler's skin began to prickle. He could see Sutter's finger tightening again on the trigger. "Warren?" Sutter asked with a little sigh, taking dead aim at Beeler's chest.

Conmy answered him with a crooked smile and a sigh of his own. "I guess you're right, Ben. You might as well get it over with."

They were going to kill him. They had just taken a vote and the verdict was unanimous. Because he no longer fitted in with their plans, they were going to shoot him and leave him for the wolves and buzzards.

Even as Beeler tensed and hurled himself to one side, he knew that it would do no good. At what was almost pointblank range, there was no chance that Sutter would miss his target. Even if he had not been an expert marksman. Beeler's was the natural action of a man trying desperately to escape sure death as it hurtled toward him.

Hopeless but natural. Ben Sutter recognized it for what it was. He smiled faintly before he fired.

When, a split second later, Beeler found himself still alive, he could not believe it. He landed face down in some scrub brush beside the deer path. Twisting and squirming, he lurched to his feet and threw himself over the rocky ledge. An instant before he fell like a rock down the sheer slope, he glimpsed Ben Sutter standing there, looking not at Beeler but at his own bloody forearm.

The only thought in Beeler's mind, as he took that sickening plunge was, *I'm not dead! Not quite yet! I'm alive!*

The picture was frozen in his brain. As he slammed and jolted down the rocky slope he could still see Sutter standing there, amazed, his rifle flying out of his hands, as if by some trick of black magic. His forearm the brilliant crimson of fresh blood. What it meant, Beeler didn't know. At the moment, he didn't care. It was enough, for the present, to be assured that he was still alive.

In his fall he crashed against a jagged outcrop and all the air went out of his lungs. He lay for a moment, stunned and gasping. *Get up!* he told himself furiously. *Get up and run!* Any second now Conmy and Sutter, and maybe Keating as well, would begin shooting him to pieces. Still, he couldn't make himself move.

A sudden burst of rifle fire shattered the moment of stillness, but amazingly no bullets tore into

Beeler's body. With agonizing slowness he turned himself over on his back. Far above him, on the ledge above the twisting deer path, Conmy and Sutter were throwing themselves at rocks or brush, whatever they could find in the way of shelter. Duane Keating had already dumped out of the saddle and was firing at something higher up in the hills.

Beeler's lungs began functioning again, and he greedily filled them with sweet, cool air. The voice inside his head was still shouting, *Run!* But for another few seconds he watched the fascinating drama up above. He saw dark puffs of gunsmoke rise lazily in the air, about a hundred yards up the slope from where Conmy and Sutter and Keating were kneeling. Slowly, everything began to come together in Beeler's mind. Somebody up there had opened fire on the hunters. Somebody had shot Sutter, nicking his forearm, an instant before he could put a bullet in Beeler's chest.

The eerily quiet and impersonal battle raged on the upper slope, but Beeler was determined to ignore it. With a change in luck, it was just possible that he might catch Keating's horse which was now nervously making its way back down the narrow deer path. That would be the end of his career as a hunting guide. Maybe the end of Elizabeth Stans's ambition to make a farmer of him, as well. But he didn't think about that now.

Run! the voice was still shouting. This time he heard and heeded it.

"What I miss most," he thought, scrambling from rock to rock along the slope, "is my rifle." It looked like everybody in these hills had a rifle, except Frank Beeler. His own weapon was still in the saddle boot, on the dun. And Lord knew where the dun had got to by this time.

Well, he consoled himself, there was still Keating's bay. If his luck was actually taking a turn for the better, there was still a chance.

The firing from above had a hesitant, thoughtful sound to it now, but Beeler did not wonder about it any more than he could help. He kept his eye on the bay. The animal of Keating's was his ticket out of these hills, out of the Nations. Out of a war that he didn't want. Most of all, out of sight and hearing of Warren Conmy and Ben Sutter!

Exactly what he was going to do when, and if, he achieved all of his immediate ambitions, he was not sure. Would anybody believe him if he told them the truth? He doubted it. And if they did believe him, nobody would sympathize with him. The Brannons, as Conmy and Sutter so liked to point out, were outlaws, after all, with bounties on their heads.

This unsatisfactory line of thought ended abruptly. Beeler, in a last-ditch effort to close the gap between himself and the bay, lowered himself into a smooth-bottomed crevasse with the hope of following the animal across the slope until their paths eventually crossed. He had taken no more than a dozen steps when the Indian materialized around the first bend.

For a few seconds the Indian only stood there, rifle cradled casually in one arm, staring at Beeler impassively. Beeler was startled. For one thing, he hadn't expected to meet anyone at all in this narrow mountain watershed, much less a broad-faced, bandy-legged little Quahada Comanche.

In typical Indian fashion, the Comanche pointed with his chin toward the upper slopes where they could still hear an occasional rifleshot. "Thee come with me."

Beeler tried to choke back his anger and frustration. In his mind he could see Keating's bay wandering farther and farther away. "Come with you where?"

For an answer the little Comanche turned his back and began walking away. Well, Beeler reasoned, he doesn't aim to kill me or he would have done it right at the beginning. He put the bay out of his mind. "Whereabouts do you think you're goin'?" he shouted at the Indian's back.

The Comanche didn't bother to answer. Instead he broke into a curiously rolling, light-footed jog, and Beeler had to stir himself to a lope in order to keep up with him. After several minutes the Indian scrambled out of the rock-floored gully and began zigzagging up the slope without once looking back to see if Beeler was following.

Beeler didn't have to think about it long. In giving up the chase of Keating's bay he had lost his best chance of escaping from his employers. His *former* employers. He decided it was better to throw in with a doubtful Comanche than to roam the hills with two proven murderers on his heels. Assuming, of course, that Conmy and Sutter got out of their present predicament alive—and there was no doubt in Beeler's mind that they would.

Beeler climbed for almost thirty minutes under the early morning sun, catching only occasional glimpses of the darting Comanche. Sweating freely, he clawed his way through thickets of stunted pine. At last the Indian appeared at the base of a towering limestone outcrop and gestured for Beeler to follow.

The Comanche and a second man were hunkered down at the base of the outcrop, idly scratching in the dirt with sticks, waiting for Beeler to finish the climb. The white man, a rifle held casually across his knees, gazed dully up at Beeler as he sagged against the rock to get his breath.

"Old John here . . ." The white man nodded at the Indian. "Old John claims you fought with the skunks that dry-gulched Rafe a while ago. Is that right?"

For several seconds Beeler didn't try to speak. He concentrated on dragging air into his tortured lungs and studying the two men who were staring up at him. The white man, from the look of his clothing, was a typical sodbuster. Rawboned, hungry-looking, tinged somehow with the aura of defeat. The Indian was everything a Comanche warrior ought to be—thick of chest, broad of face, with short, bowed legs for the Quahada brand of daredevil horsemanship. His heavy black braids lay on his chest; a cast-off cavalry hat was pulled squarely down on his head.

With all the life-and-death questions whirling in Beeler's mind, all he could think to say was, "I guess it's none of my business, but would somebody tell me what a Comanche's doin' here in the Choctaw hills?"

The white man chuckled approvingly. "You know your redskins, all right. This here's John Coyotesong. Went to a Quaker school over on the reservation when he was just a sprout; talks American as good as you or me. John's the one that saved your hide. Shot the rifle out of that buzzard's hands clean as a blackbird peckin' corn. John," he confessed with a wry grin, "is the only man in the bunch that's worth a damn with a rifle."

Beeler took a second, closer look at the little Indian. "John," he said with a good deal of feeling, "I'm much obliged for the way you sat in and dealt yourself a hand. If there's ever anything I can do for you, there's a favor you got comin'."

The Comanche shrugged and looked totally indifferent to what anyone, a white man least of all, might think about him.

There was a moment of silence while the white man's naturally long face grew even longer. "Tell you the truth," he went on quietly, "it wasn't that John was so anxious to do you a favor. Rafe Jackson was his pal; they been ridin' together ever since the big dry-up last year when me and Leo had to leave the farm." He paused and spat thoughtfully into the dirt. "Rafe was scoutin' our backtrail, like he always does in the mornin'. Me and John was lookin' after the horses when we heard the shot, but when we got to where we could see what was goin' on, Rafe was already spread out in the dust and them two coyotes was standin' over him. Then you came along and, best we could tell, seemed like you was takin' Rafe's part. Ain't that about the way it happened?"

"Just about," Beeler nodded. "Do you mind if I ask a question?"

The Comanche shrugged. The white man said, "Go ahead."

"Are you boys part of the Brannon bunch?"

Both men looked at him in surprise. "I'll be damned! How'd you know?"

"It's on the telegraph about how you robbed the Katy and rode off with forty thousand dollars in a strongbox."

The white man groaned, as if the memory of that

robbery caused him considerable pain. "Mister," he said, "you're right now lookin' at the whole damn Brannon gang. Except for Leo. He's up there on the ridge keepin' an eye on things." Beeler turned and looked at the distant ridge and was vaguely disturbed to see the rifleman looking down at them. "I'm Babe," the man said. "Me and Leo're brothers."

"I had just about guessed that much," Beeler told him dryly. "You and Leo must be the most famous brothers in the Territory by this time."

Both Babe and the little Comanche looked startled. "You sure we're talkin' about the same Brannons?"

"I'm talkin' about the Brannons that held up the Katy two days ago. The Brannons that robbed the bank in the Cherokee Nation. And another train in Kansas."

Babe's mouth fell open in amazement. "How'd you know all them things?"

"Like I said, it's all on the telegraph. Everybody knows. Besides that, there's considerable bounty on your heads; one thousand dollars for Leo, five hundred for the others."

Babe Brannon began to look alarmed. "Hell," he complained, "we never figgered on anything like *that!* Just a few farm boys tryin' to make ends meet durin' hard times; didn't hardly seem like we'd be important enough to get put on the telegraph."

"A bunch that steals forty thousand dollars at a crack," Beeler told him, "is considered important to some folks."

"Mister," the outlaw said passionately, "if I was to tell you about that forty thousand dollars you wouldn't believe me." Suddenly he lurched to his feet and waved his hat to the figure on the ridge. "We'll get Leo down here and talk this over. One thing we never counted on in this outlawin' business, and that was bein' famous!"

As they waited for the outlaw leader to come down from the ridge, Beeler began to get the feeling that solid ground was giving away beneath his feet. There was something ridiculous about learning that the notorious Brannon gang actually amounted to two bumbling farm boys and a strayed Comanche. The mere fact that he should be here talking to them was bizarre and tainted with unreality.

They heard the clatter of heavy brogan shoes coming down the rocky path. When Leo Brannon came into view Beeler was not surprised to see that he was a slightly older, slightly more dejected copy of his brother, Babe. The outlaw cut himself a small chew of tobacco and looked dully at Beeler. "Your pals are gone," he said grimly. "Caught their horses and lit out. Took your dun, too. I guess that leaves you here afoot."

"They're not exactly pals of mine," Beeler told him. In some detail he explained about the hunting party and how he had got the job of guiding it, but he had the feeling that Leo wasn't listening to half of it.

"Why," the outlaw asked abruptly, "did they kill Rafe?"

"There's bounty on our heads," Babe said excitedly—and he seemed to be a man who didn't get excited very often. "A thousand dollars for you, five hundred for the rest of us!"

Beeler shook his head. He didn't know how he was going to explain this to them, but he knew that he had to try. "It wasn't the money; they've already got plenty of that. With them it's . . . kind of a game."

"A game?" Babe frowned.

"The man that killed your friend is Ben Sutter. He and Warren Conmy are rich boys with nothin' much to do, I guess. So they gamble. They make bets with each other . . ." He could see that he wasn't getting through. He told them about the turkey slaughter. About throwing knives at a mark on the hotel door. "Well," he went on, "this time their game is huntin' outlaws—the famous Brannons. I'm not acquainted with all the details, but I think they aim to hunt you down and kill you one by one. The way I figger it, they've put a number to each outlaw. A bigger number for Leo, the leader, a smaller number for the others. When all of you are dead, the game is over; the one with the biggest score is the winner."

The three outlaws stared at him in chilled fascination. "There's men that play *games* with other men's lives? It's not even for the money?"

"That's the way I understand it."

"Them two dudes!" Babe Brannon scowled fiercely. "They must be loco!"

Beeler shrugged. "Whatever they are, they're dangerous. Your friend Rafe Jackson is already dead. The game has started, and Sutter is leading. It'll be Conmy's next move; and he won't waste any time tryin' to catch up."

"But they headed out of the hills. I seen them."

"They'll be back." Beeler didn't know just how he could be so sure of this, but he was. "And there's not just the two of them. There's Keating—you saw him with me. And there's a butler back at camp." He didn't try to explain what a butler was. "They're all well mounted, well armed, and they're dead shots."

There was enough in that thought to give the outlaws pause. No one had to tell them that they were poorly mounted, poorly armed, and, with the exception of John Coyotesong, they were poor shots. For once, Leo decided to act instead of wait and see. "Boys," he said soberly, "when it comes to dollar-a-day possemen and deputy marshals, I know pretty much what to expect. But I ain't had a whole lot of experience in bein' hunted for sport. Gettin' shot down from ambush, like poor Rafe Jackson." He shook his head several times, looking bewildered and a little frightened. “Most likely they ain’t goin’ to come back. But in case they do, we better break camp and get us another place to hide.”

“You mind a little company?” Beeler asked with a crooked grin.

Leo thought about this for a minute. “Why,” he asked, “would you want to throw in with us, if them dudes are as dangerous as you say?”

“I’ve got a strong hunch that Conmy and Sutter have changed the rules of their game by this time. I’m part of the total score now, if my guess is right.” He wondered what kind of number they would give him. As high as Leo’s? Maybe even higher?

“There’s one thing I’d like to know,” Babe Brannon said. “Why did you fly into that dude after he shot Rafe? Rafe didn’t mean anything to you.”

Beeler shrugged. “He was a man.”

They buried Rafe in the rocks near the deer path and immediately began pushing toward the higher ridges to the east. Toward midafternoon John Coyotesong found a cave on one of the highest peaks overlooking Black Fork Creek. “Black Fork Hill,” Leo said, indicating a hazy peak in the distance. “Arkansas.”

They gazed to the east without enthusiasm. Arkansas meant federal courts and deputy marshals—they would rather take their chances in the

Choctaw Nation. "John," Leo told the Comanche, "you take a look at our backtrail and make sure there ain't nobody trackin' us."

Beeler and Babe Brannon sat on the ground and rubbed their aching feet. They listened to the howl of the wind as it moved through the dense stands of pine. Leo stripped his saddle animal, set it out to graze, and then inspected the cave. "Well," he reported on his return, "it ain't much of a home, but I reckon it'll have to do."

John Coyotesong returned from his scout and reported no sign of Conmy or Sutter. The outlaws cheered up slightly. "There ain't nobody ever goin' to find us in this cave," Leo assured them.

"What I wish we had," Babe Brannon sighed, "is some decent grub."

What they had for supper was what they'd had for dinner, leather-tough jerky and pale coffee boiled from week-old Arbuckle's grounds.

"I can't help wonderin'," Beeler said at last, "just how you boys got into the outlawin' business in the first place."

Babe Brannon shrugged. "There ain't nothin' queer about it. When me and Leo lost the farm, it seemed like outlawin' was about the only thing left to try. We didn't figger to take it up as a regular thing. A few months, maybe, till we got back on our feet." He heaved a rueful sigh. "I guess it didn't work out just the way we figgered."

"John," Beeler asked the little Comanche,

"how'd a Plains Indian come to get hooked with train robbin'?"

John Coyotesong chewed his jerky impassively. "Better," he said at last, "than farmin'."

If Beeler hadn't been so footsore and tired he could have laughed. A less-promising bunch of outlaws he had never seen—the Brannons, who had taken to robbing trains because they had lost their farm, and John Coyotesong, who had joined them because of Quaker Indian agents who were trying to *make* him farm. "I guess it ain't any of my business," Beeler told them solemnly, "but if I was in your place I think I'd look for another line of work."

CHAPTER SIX

The next day Beeler climbed the rock-capped ridge overlooking the cave and studied the paths leading down from the hills. Far to the north was the old Fort Smith–Washita military road, but he didn't give himself much chance of reaching it without a horse. The way east was more attractive—it would be a long, hard climb, but at the end of it there would be old friends in Arkansas. He considered the area to the south only briefly—the way down to the Kiamichi valley was too rough and too far for a foot traveler. To the west the chances of running into Conmy and Sutter were too great. "Without a rifle," he told himself grimly, "I want to give that pair plenty of room."

East, toward Arkansas, still seemed his best chance. He no longer thought of them as outlaws—they were friends, with common enemies in Conmy and Sutter. All the same, he wasn't sure how they would accept his escape to a land swarming with deputy marshals. A man without a horse or a job, or even a rifle, maybe he would decide to come back with a posse and collect some of that bounty money.

Beeler grinned to himself. Definitely, the best thing was to leave without a word.

It was early afternoon when he scrambled down the back side of the cave and began his long climb toward the Black Fork Mountains. Within a short time he had raised a blister on his left foot and was limping badly. By midafternoon his boot was sticky with blood. He looked back over his shoulder in the direction of the cave and wondered if he was doing the right thing after all.

For a moment he paused to get his breath and listen to the stillness of that wooded slope. "Wonder where they are?" he thought out loud. Not the outlaws. Conmy and Sutter. Maybe they had given up their bloody little game in favor of some other amusement. But he didn't think so. Warren Conmy and Ben Sutter were definitely not the kind to knock off and leave a diversion unfinished.

High on one of the northern ridges a bit of metal caught the sun and spat it out in a flash of light. Beeler watched the spot for several minutes, but the light did not reappear. Maybe, he thought, it hadn't been metal at all. A piece of mica in one of the rocks, most likely.

He took up the climb again without removing his boot. There was a sweaty coldness on the back of his neck that hadn't been there before.

He climbed for another hour, then paused for breath. He wondered how long it would take him to get to Arkansas. Three days at least, at the rate he was going. Then it would probably take the best part of the fourth day to find help.

"Exactly what kind of help am I lookin' for?"

he asked himself. "Some lawmen to get a posse and look for the Brannons?" No. He didn't care about the Brannons. What he did care about was Conmy and Sutter. What I'd really like to do, he thought bitterly, is get a posse together and go after *them.*

It was somewhere in the middle of that thought that the bullet struck him. At first it was hardly more than a nick—a slight tug at his shoulder. He even glimpsed a tiny piece of his shirt fly into the air. Then the bee sting on his upper arm. And blood.

"By God," he found himself saying aloud, "the bastards are tryin' to kill me!"

Not for an instant did it occur to him that the shot might have come from one of the outlaws. The range was too great, for one thing. The outlaws were not equipped with the rifles or the marksmanship that this kind of shooting required. *Conmy!* The name flashed in his mind even as he threw himself down the rocky slope.

The distant report of a rifle was flattened and swallowed up in the dense timber. Beeler found himself on his hands and knees scrambling frantically from bush to outcrop to a fallen oak. He fell behind the rotting trunk, his heart racing wildly. Now he knew how the rabbit felt with the hounds just a jump away.

A sudden hush fell over those hills of jumbled rock and timber. What was Conmy doing now?

Paying his bet? What was Sutter doing? Adding up the score? Laughing?

A breeze whispered down from the north. The hills sighed.

Then there was sudden movement on the ridge. It was Conmy, impatient, angry, unwilling to believe that he could have missed his target two times running.

"You've got to get up from here," Beeler told himself. "Start runnin' and keep on runnin'. A movin' target's harder to hit. Start runnin' before they get any closer. The next time he won't miss."

With great reluctance he shoved himself up from the momentary safety of the fallen oak. *Run!* He threw himself down the rocky grade, tearing through brush, tripping over vines and outcrops, stumbling, falling. He collapsed at the base of a great live-oak tree and lay gasping. Now he knew why he had allowed Elizabeth to talk him into quitting the law-enforcement business—it was young man's work, and he was no longer young.

He could hear Conmy and Sutter, still far up the slope, as they threw caution to the winds. They came romping down the slope, dodging in and out between the trees, whooping and laughing like youngsters on a Sunday outing. *Laughing!* Well, Beeler thought grimly, let's just see how funny this strikes you. He drew his .45, braced it steadily against the tree, and waited for them to come into sight.

Conmy was the first to show himself. He burst out of a dense undergrowth and stood for a moment on a little knoll. Beeler centered him precisely in his sights. The range he judged at about one hundred yards—much too great for the revolver—but there was a kind of fierce satisfaction in just seeing the young hunter there in front of his muzzle. Closer, Mr. Conmy! Come just a little closer!

Conmy was smiling widely. His eyes were bright with satisfaction. He turned and waved his rifle to Sutter, who was showing more caution than his friend and had taken up a position in the timber. "I think I see where he fell, Ben! Don't shoot, this one belongs to me!"

A clammy sweat formed on Beeler's forehead. As Conmy started down the slope, Beeler kept him centered with the front sight of his .45. *Closer!* he thought in a cold fury.

Then, completely unexpectedly, a rifle bellowed from the high ground somewhere to Beeler's right. A bullet kicked up a small shower of leaves at Conmy's feet. The rifle crashed a second time, and this time Conmy betrayed alarm. For a moment he appeared to be stunned, not knowing where to turn. The unseen rifle sounded a third time; almost immediately a small spot of crimson marred the perfection of Conmy's Bedford-cord trousers. From his position in the timber, Sutter opened fire, and Beeler was forced to admire the cool and deadly precision with which he peppered the hillside with a rain of lead.

Conmy, looking wild now and pale with fright, turned and reeled back toward the timber. He limped as he ran, but not badly. A halfway decent rifleman could have dropped Conmy with the first shot. Which meant that the shooting must have been the work of one of the Brannon brothers.

Beeler watched resignedly as Conmy staggered into the dense undergrowth and disappeared. For a little while there was no movement and no sound. Sutter was putting a bandage on Conmy's wound, Beeler decided. After several minutes he heard the sound of horses making their way north.

Beeler sat at the base of the live oak in a cold rage. After an attempt at cold-blooded murder, Conmy and Sutter were getting away scot free. The nick that Conmy had received didn't matter. Within a day, or probably less, he would be in the saddle again. With murder in his heart.

Beeler was not in a mood to be grateful when Babe Brannon appeared ambling down the opposite slope, casually swinging his rifle at his side as if it were a club. As he came up the grade to where Beeler was still sitting, the former lawman asked coldly, "Are you actually that rotten a shot, or did you miss that killer on purpose?"

Babe rested his rifle against the live oak and looked at him blandly. "Can't say as I did it a purpose," he said, "but this old gun of mine shies off to the high side, and sometimes I forget." He hunkered down beside Beeler and helped himself to a small bite of plug tobacco. "If you don't mind me askin', whereabouts do you think you was goin', before all the shootin' started?"

There didn't seem to be much point in lying about it. "I figgered I'd make for Arkansas."

"And then what?"

"I don't know. Nothin', I guess." He tied his bandana around the shallow wound in his arm.

"Nothin' . . ." Babe chewed on the word for a while. "I ain't sure I believe you, mister. The way you sneaked off from camp. And takin' into consideration all that money that's on our heads. Can you tell me for sure that you wasn't aimin' to fetch yourself some help and collect some of that bounty?"

Had that thought been in the back of his mind? Beeler couldn't be sure. But he didn't think so. He shrugged and tried to smile wryly. "I don't know. Maybe that's what I'd of done."

Surprisingly, Babe Brannon grinned. "You still set on the notion of makin' for Arkansas?"

In his mind Beeler could still see the excitement of the hunt in Warren Conmy's eyes. The wide grin, the godlike smugness. Well, he thought angrily, it's about time he learned he's not God! "Babe, if it's all the same to you, I think I'll change my mind and stay with you boys a while."

“Even if it means gettin’ a price slapped on your head?”

“Even if it means that.”

Babe shrugged. “It’s all right with me. But there’s one thing that makes me wonder. It’s a hard, long climb to the Black Fork Mountains—have you got pals over there?”

Beeler hesitated only a moment. “One way or another,” he said. “I guess you’d find out. I used to ride for the court at Fort Smith.”

The outlaw whistled softly. “You rode for old Hangin’ Judge Parker? What do you reckon he’s goin’ to say when he finds out one of his boys has took up with the Brannons?”

“That,” Beeler told him in all honesty, “is somethin’ I’d rather not think about right now.”

Babe appeared to accept that as an explanation. After a moment he asked, “You figger them two dudes’ll come after us again?”

“That’s what I figger. You shot one of them, but it was just a nick in the leg. He’ll be back in the saddle tomorrow, good and mad. If I was Leo, I’d think about movin’ camp again.”

At the camp on the bank of Brushy Creek, Warren Conmy lay in a cold rage while his wife and Humphrey O’Toole dressed his wound. Nearby, Ben Sutter watched with an air of mild amusement. “You’ve got to admit,” he said with a grin, “that with Beeler on the other side, it makes for a more interesting hunt." Giving Beeler an active role in their "game" had been Ben's idea. Conmy had gone along reluctantly. It wasn't "sporting," he had argued, to change the rules of the game after they had once been established and the game underway. However, in the end Beeler had sealed his own doom by striking Conmy. To Sutter's knowledge, no man had ever struck Warren Conmy without living to regret it.

With surprising efficiency, Verna Conmy cleaned her husband's wound with soap and water. Then swabbed it with coal oil and bound it with a piece of his own linen shirt. She looked at him, smiling and shaking her head, like an adoring mother gently reproving a precocious child. "Warren, you've simply got to be more careful. Mr. Beeler is an experienced lawman and you've got to make allowances. Ben," she told her brother, "I want you to promise that this sort of foolishness will not happen again."

Ben Sutter shrugged good-naturedly. "You know how Warren is when a bet is down."

"Next time," she said with mock sternness, "take Duane with you. I insist." She looked up and smiled brilliantly at Keating. "Duane, will you do that, as a special favor to me? Keep an eye on Ben and Warren and see that they do nothing foolish?"

Duane Keating looked slightly dazed, as he always did when Verna Conmy smiled at him. "Of course," he said after clearing his throat. "If Ben and Warren will allow it, that is."

"They'll allow it. Because I insist." She placed a sympathetic hand on her husband's forehead. "It's a shallow wound; I don't think there'll be much soreness. But I want you to stay out of the saddle for a day. There's no hurry; the game won't go on without you."

"No," Conmy said shortly, in a tone that he rarely used with his beautiful wife. "There'll be no waiting. Tomorrow at first light the game will resume."

Verna sighed resignedly.

After one of O'Toole's cold suppers they sat around a shielded campfire and listened to the rustling night sounds in the timber. The hills to the east loomed high and rugged. Warren was still angry with Ben for having pulled him away from the fight and bringing him back to camp. "It was a mistake to break it off today," he said accusingly to his brother-in-law.

"I doubt it," Ben said with a shrug. "The last I saw of Beeler he looked ready and eager to rejoin forces with the outlaws. Don't worry, they're not going to get away from us."

The next morning O'Toole set a breakfast of Virginia ham and the last of the fresh eggs. The day was sparkling clean and smelled of dew. Ben Sutter stretched luxuriously and smiled toward the hills. "A fine day ahead of us. With a little luck we ought to finish it before sundown."

"If we can find them again," Conmy said sourly. "No doubt they've moved their camp, after what happened yesterday."

Sutter smiled with extravagant self-assurance. "We'll find them. If not tomorrow, the next day."

Duane Keating brought up the horses and got them saddled. If he resented being treated as a stableboy, he didn't show it. "Everything's ready, Warren," he said, holding the stirrup for his boss.

A bright edge of golden sun showed itself above the eastern ridges. Keating continued to patiently hold the stirrup while Conmy kissed his wife. "We may not be back till tomorrow, Verna. Don't worry, Hump will take good care of you."

"Are you sure you feel like riding?"

Conmy showed his irritation at being treated like an invalid. "I feel fine. Duane, hold that bay steady, can't you?"

Perhaps Ben Sutter noticed that Keating's face became strangely stiff, but no one else seemed to. "Duane . . ." Verna Conmy reached out and touched the secretary. "Take good care of my brother and my husband."

"Everything's going to be fine, Verna. Don't worry."

O'Toole's face became beet red and he chuckled to himself at the thought of a Conmy or a Sutter depending on anyone at all—much less Keating—for their safety. It was only because of Verna that they were allowing the secretary to go with them.

As the three men reined east and headed for the dark, rock-capped hills, Verna stood in front of her tent, waving and smiling. So many times before she had watched them ride off this way, hunting lion or the murderous buffalo in the jungles of East Africa, the quick-killing puma of Wyoming, bear in California. But this time it was not quite the same—they had never gone hunting men before.

A little thrill of uneasiness swept over her. "Hump . . . are they going to be all right?"

"Of course they'll be all right, ma'am. They're expert shots; none better. Their rifles are the best the Marlin people can make."

"But they've never gone on a hunt like this one before."

"A hunt's a hunt, ma'am. Don't worry about that pair, they'll be fine."

John Coyotesong returned from his morning scout and reported three horsebackers entering the hills from the west. "It just don't seem fair," Leo Brannon complained, "that we have to contend with a pack of sportin' dudes, on top of deputy marshals and possemen!"

"Three of them this time," Beeler said, thinking out loud. "Babe, looks like that nick of yours threw a scare into Conmy. Anyway, the third rider will be either Keating or O'Toole— they're both dead shots. Most likely it's Keating."

“We still got them outnumbered four to three,” Babe put in.

“What we’ve got is one pistol and three rifles that can’t be trusted to hit anything fifty yards away. They’ve got the guns and the marksmanship to kill at three hundred yards—maybe further, if they have telescopic sights.”

John Coyotesong smiled coldly, remembering his friend Rafe Jackson. “Ambush.”

Leo nodded slowly. “We could try it. The four of us sure can’t do much runnin’ with just two horses.”

Beeler’s tone turned dry. “There’s somethin’ we better think about. If we lay a successful ambush, the world outside these hills will call it murder. Conmy and Sutter come from rich and powerful families; if anything happens to them you can expect these hills to soon be swarmin’ with deputy marshals and private bounty hunters.”

Leo’s mouth turned down and began to tremble, as if he might actually start crying at the unfairness of it all. “Why would they go and do a thing like *that?* Them dudes are tryin’ to murder *us,* ain’t they?”

“*We* know it, but nobody else does.” Beeler shook his head. “No, our best chance is to run. If we lay the ambush we’ll have to answer for murder.”

Actually it wasn’t so much the charge of murder

that worried Beeler; he knew instinctively that any sort of ambush that involved the Brannons was sure to fail, just as everything else they had tried had failed. "No," he repeated, "what we've got to do is run."

"What," Babe asked bitterly, "do you aim to use for horses?"

John Coyotesong pointed lazily to the south. "Horses down there."

They stared at him. "What horses?" Beeler asked. "What're you talkin' about?"

"Choctaws. Four horses, wagon."

"What are they doin' up here in the hills?"

The little Comanche shrugged and smiled bleakly. Members of the Civilized Tribes were as foreign to him as white men, and sometimes more so. "A hunting party, maybe," Beeler said slowly. "Or maybe it's just a family travelin' cross country to see some kinfolks." With growing larceny in his heart, he grinned at John Coyotesong. "Four horses, you say. We could kind of borrow two and leave two. It wouldn't hardly be like settin' them completely afoot."

Leo Brannon was looking at the Comanche with profound disgust. "Goddammit, John, why didn't you *tell* us about them Choctaws?"

"Thee didn't ask. Anyway, stealin' horses from Indians not easy."

"It'll have to be done. Ain't Comanches supposed to be the biggest horse thieves on the plains?"

John allowed himself a small smile of pride. "Break camp. We get started quick before they move."

It was early afternoon when they raised the small camp of Choctaws on one of the deep branches of the Kiamichi. Four ponies, as John had said, sleek and fat on summer grass.

Three Indians sat around a fire cooking squirrels on a spit. The horses were hobbled and grazing peacefully a short distance downstream. It was a peaceful scene—almost too peaceful to be true.

Beeler and the outlaws lay in a redbud thicket looking down on the campsite. "There ain't but three of them," Leo said. "I don't see no reason why we couldn't throw down on them, take the animals and ride off."

"Hold on a minute . . ." Beeler squinted hard at the three figures slumped by the fire. "Somethin's queer here." His lawman's nose could almost smell it. It didn't actually look like a camp at all; nothing had been taken out of the wagon. The Indians were just sitting there waiting. Waiting for what?

Suddenly he broke into a wide grin. "Boys, what you're lookin' at down there is three drunk Choctaws. I bet if you was to raise that tarp and look in the wagon you'd see a hundred half-gallon jars of corn whiskey. We've blundered into a nest of whiskey runners."

One by one the outlaws began to grin. "By God," Leo said happily, "I think you're right. Wonder where they come from?"

"Up from Texas, most likely. I figger they're just the haulers, and this is the meetin' place where they sell their load to honkey-tonk owners and other dealers. I guess they got tired waitin' for customers and decided to sample some of their own stock."

Babe Brannon chuckled. "Lucky day for us to start in the horse-stealin' business."

Only John Coyotesong failed to look happy at this unexpected turn of events. Horse stealing was supposed to be dangerous and exciting sport—it was almost as if those three Choctaws had deliberately let him down.

All the time they had been watching, the Indians had sat like three lumps of stone, unmoving. The scent of charred squirrel floated up to them; they hadn't even bothered to turn the meat on the spit. "Babe," Beeler grinned, "let's me and you go and catch us some saddle animals to ride; I've might near had a bait of walkin'."

Leo and John Coyotesong remained in the redbud thicket with their rifles. Beeler and Babe quietly slipped around the edge of the camp, unhobbled a mouse dun and a roan—both stallions—and led them away. The Indians continued to sit slumped over like sacks of oats while their dinner burned on the spit. Everything went so well that Babe and Beeler returned for the bridles and saddles that were lying where the animals had been stripped. Up in the redbud thicket John Coyotesong uttered a sound of disgust.

"Well," Beeler thought to himself, "now I'm a real outlaw. A horse thief." But he didn't let it bother him. "Boys," he told the nodding Choctaws silently, "if losin' a pair of saddle animals is the worst you ever get for haulin' whiskey, consider yourselves lucky."

The outlaws regrouped upstream from the Indian camp to decide what to do next. Beeler, now the owner of a strong roan stallion and a passable single-shot saddle, again began to think about the advantages of Arkansas.

Leo Brannon read his mind. "If you want to go . . ." The outlaw spread his hands fatalistically. "I guess we understand how you feel. There ain't no future in gettin' yourself tied to a bunch of hard time outlaws with prices on their heads. Never mind that Babe saved your life. When them two lobos was about to fix you up for buryin'." The outlaw leader pulled a sorrowful face and made it sound as if his best friend had just shot him in the back.

There was just a chance—a small one, Beeler thought, but a chance—that there was something in the claim that Babe had kept Conmy from killing him. "Leo," he said reasonably, "I'd be more of a hindrance to you than anything else. If we ran into deputy marshals I'd have to take their part, not yours. As for Conmy and Sutter, you've got horses and guns, you'll have to deal with them the best way you can."

"Horses and guns." Leo smiled sadly. "They can kill at three hundred yards, maybe farther. You said so yourself. And us . . . well, you seen how we shoot. They'll pick us off one at a time until we're all gone . . . unless, that is, you was to take it in your head to help us."

How the Brannons had ever got to be notorious outlaws, Beeler would never understand. "Leo," he said patiently, "there ain't any way I can help you."

"You used to ride the Nations as a lawman. Don't you know somebody that would put us up until folks kind of forget about the Brannons?"

"No."

But this was not quite the whole truth, and Leo saw that it wasn't. A deputy marshal didn't ride a territory for five years without building up a list of personal debts and credits. There were people who were obligated to him for one reason or another—but could he reasonably ask them to give shelter and comfort to a bunch of wanted outlaws?

"Somethin's goin' around in your head," Leo accused him. "I can see it."

"It's nothin', Leo. It wouldn't work. Besides, it's too far."

The outlaw brightened. "How far?"

"All the way to the Three Fork country, in the

Creek Nation. You'd never make it without runnin' into federal lawmen, or at least Conmy and Sutter."

"Think about this for a minute," Babe Brannon put in. "How much chance are we goin' to have if we stay where we are?"

Beeler didn't have to think about it. The three of them would not last a day against Conmy and Sutter, once those "sportsmen" got on their trail. They were no match for Conmy's cold-bloodedness and Sutter's skill. But the feel of a strong horse between his legs gave Beeler a fresh outlook; he figured that his own chances, alone, were good. If necessary he could call in personal debts. He could go to old friends of the court for protection. A man of his experience, with a good horse to ride, had little to fear from men like Conmy and Sutter and their deadly little game.

But only if he was alone. In company with the Brannons the situation became dangerous. Old friends would become enemies. Men who were obligated to Beeler would forget their obligations and see only the bounty on the outlaws' heads. No, he thought, that would not do. When a man turned outlaw he had to take his chances. The Brannons must have known that when they started the business.

"There are places," he told Leo, "where outlaws can go and stay out of sight for a while. You must know some; you've been in the business long enough for that."

The outlaw's grin had a bitter twist. "There's places right here in the Nations that I've heard about. All a body wants is money."

If they emptied their pockets, Beeler thought wryly, I bet they couldn't get together a dollar amongst the three of them. "The best I can do," he said reluctantly, "is tell you a man's name. You can tell him I sent you, and it might be he'll help you; he owes me a favor. On the other hand, he might not; he's an Indian and might not want to stir up trouble."

"Hell's afire," Leo beamed, as if all his problems had been magically solved, "old John here's a Indian. They'll get along fine. What's your pal's name?"

"Hooker. Duel Hooker. He'll be at the Three Forks Meetin' House; that shouldn't be hard to find."

They stared at him. "Meetin' House?"

Beeler smiled wanly. "Hooker's a Baptist preacher, and for all I know he's chalked me off as a soul not worth savin' any more. But the way I see it, he's about the only hope you've got."

The Brannon brothers thought this over for a moment. "Hell," Leo said at last, "I don't reckon we've got anything to lose. Boys, what we best do is get ourselves headed back towards Creek country and get things settled with Brother Hooker."

Beeler smiled doubtfully. "I can't guarantee he'll help."

“He’ll help, all right.” Leo chuckled, riding the crest of one of his happy moods. “I can feel it in my bones. You sure you don’t want to come along?”

“I’m sure.”

“Will you be headin’ back to the Oklahoma country?” Babe asked.

“I guess.” Although he didn’t know what he would do there. With no money, no credit, there would be no homestead and no Elizabeth. That thought left him strangely unmoved. He was beginning to think that he had never much wanted to be a farmer anyway.

CHAPTER SEVEN

All that day Duane Keating had been riding a respectful length behind Conmy and Sutter. His face was gray with dust kicked up by their horses. Whenever they stopped to inspect the trail, or to take a drink of water, Keating was the first one out of the saddle to do their bidding. "Fetch me that canteen, Duane. Hurry up, Duane, what takes you so long?"

It hadn't always been that way. Once they had been equals, rich and privileged kids riding their own ponies while other youngsters walked barefoot in the dust. But somewhere along the line the balance of wealth, and the respect that went with it, had shifted. Perhaps his father had been weak; all he knew was that one day the Keating Packing Company was the Conmy-Sutter Packing Company. Suddenly his contest with Warren for the affections of Ben's sister was no contest at all; by the time Warren was fourteen it was well known that one day he and Verna Sutter would be married.

Duane's father, before he died, had sought to comfort his son by assuring him an education in the best universities—there was enough left of the Keating fortune for that. But his expensive education had been of little help. In the end he had been drawn back to Chicago, because that was where

Verna was. In the end, the four of them had re-formed their old childhood circle, but with a difference. Now Verna was Mrs. Warren Conmy, and Duane was her husband's employee.

"Duane, bring that canteen up here; have you gone to sleep in the saddle?"

Keating kneed his bay up the threadlike deer path and handed Warren the saddle canteen. Earlier that afternoon they had discovered a cave that had been recently occupied. Conmy and Sutter had scouted the area until they picked up hoofmarks on the rocky ground. "South," Ben Sutter said. "Wonder why they would be heading south?"

Ben dumped out of the saddle and studied the tracks for some time. "Looks like two riding, two walking." He grinned. "With luck we'll have it finished before sundown."

"At least the score will be evened," Conmy promised coldly. "Duane, I hope you thought to bring the telescope."

"Here in the saddlebag," Keating told him.

"Take good care of it. I've got a feeling I'll be using it before long."

But the trail south had been steep and treacherous, and the pain from his wound had rubbed Warren's temper raw. It was now an hour short of sundown, and he was spitting venom, most of it aimed at Keating. However, the tracks were still clear and seemed to be leading them down to a branch of the Kiamichi. At last Ben said, “Stay here, Warren, and rest your leg. I’ll scout ahead as far as the river.”

Sutter was gone for almost half an hour, and then returned with a crooked grin. “They’ve been this way, all right. There’s a camp of drunk Indians down there running in circles looking for lost horses. Best I could make out, Beeler and the Brannons came in and stole the horses while the Indians were too drunk to know what was happening.”

Conmy flew into a rage. “They’re all mounted now, and Lord knows how far they’ve gone! Why didn’t you get back sooner?”

“Settle down,” his brother-in-law told him calmly. “I followed their trail a little way out of the riverbottom. It looks like they’re doubling back on themselves and heading north again.”

Conmy cocked his head thoughtfully. North. With luck they could swim the river before sundown and still cut them off. “Duane,” he said sharply, “get that telescope ready.”

The river was swift and icy but not deep; as they crossed it the sun was just touching the higher peaks in the west. “Twenty minutes, maybe another half an hour of light,” Ben Sutter said. “We may have to wait and pick up the trail tomorrow.”

“No!” Conmy snarled. “They can’t have gotten far if they headed north from the river.”

They put their horses up the steep slope from the river; their shadows lay black and cold on the green grass; the air was still. Suddenly Sutter reined his animal up and pointed. "There you are, Warren. Three of them, anyhow."

The three outlaws had just gained the high ground on the opposite slope and were moving slowly along the bright edge of the sky. In the harsh, direct light of the sun, their metal buckles and bit-chains glittered. Warren judged the distance at three hundred yards. Almost no wind. "Give me that glass," he said to Keating.

The secretary quickly uncased the four-power German telescope and handed it to Conmy. "Cut me a fork," Conmy snapped, without bothering to look around.

His face burning ever so slightly, Keating got down and cut a forked rest stick from a wild-plum sapling. In the meantime Conmy had dismounted and fixed the scope to the brackets of his rifle. He took the rest stick from Keating without comment, rested the rifle in the fork, and looked quickly through the glass. "Three hundred I make it," he said to Sutter.

Ben nodded.

"No wind to speak of." Conmy made the necessary adjustments and took a deep breath. The face of the lead rider leaped into the glass. "I'll be damned," he thought, an instant before squeezing the trigger. "It's an Indian."

John Coyotesong died the same way his friend Rafe Jackson had died, suddenly, silently, without knowing what had hit him. Leo Brannon, riding directly behind the little Comanche, stared dumbly as John pitched suddenly to the off side of his pony. Only when he was almost out of the saddle did Leo and Babe hear the shot.

"Goddamn!" Babe blurted. He kicked his animal brutally and reined downhill. Leo did the same an instant before a second bullet nicked a piece from the cantle of his saddle. At last the two brothers reined up at the bottom of the grade, their faces pale, their hearts fluttering in panic. They stared up at the ridge where John's pony was racing in frightened circles, dragging the Comanche's body with one foot in the stirrup.

Leo wiped the back of a trembling hand across his mouth. "I figger old John's past helpin'."

Babe took a deep, ragged breath. "Maybe. But it goes against the grain to just ride off and leave him."

They sat for a while with the crest of the hill between them and the assassin. John's pony dragged the body down the slope a way where it finally rolled free. "I guess you're right," Leo said at last. "We owe John better'n that. Anyhow, them dry gulchers are over on the other side of the slope; I guess they ain't goin' to come over here for a little while."

They led their own animals back up the grade;

the Comanche's pony had already disappeared on the far side of the hill.

When the two brothers reached the body they stood there for several seconds. "John?" Leo said meaninglessly. The little Indian lay there like a sad rag doll, his old cavalry hat missing, his heavy braids spread out like dark wings on the grass.

"What do you aim to do?" Babe asked at last.

Leo shook his head, his eyes slightly glazed. "I don't know. I just don't know."

"Maybe we ought to head back to that Choctaw camp and see if they would help. After all, old John was a Indian."

"A Comanche. That's a long way from a Choctaw. Anyhow, I don't figger they're goin' to be in any big hurry to help the bunch that stole their horses."

"You figger we could find Beeler again? He's had experience at this kind of thing."

"Beeler's gone to Arkansas," Babe sighed. "And I can't say that I blame him."

Once the sun slipped behind the hills darkness came quickly. Babe and Leo lifted John Coyotesong's body with strange gentleness and put it across Leo's saddle. Leo sighed. "I kind of wish old John had hauled his rifle out of the boot before his pony got away. It was the only decent gun of the bunch."

But the rifle and spare ammunition were gone

with the pony, and the notorious Brannon gang had been reduced to two. The brothers had been walking and leading for several minutes when Babe asked, "Have you got any notion where we're goin'?"

"We got to find us a place with some protection to it. I don't want to get caught in the open by them dry gulchers."

"It's dark. They can't do us much damage now, even with telescopes. Maybe we ought to start figgerin' what we're goin' to do with old John."

Leo heaved another of his enormous sighs. "Wonder if the Comanche had any kinfolks?"

"He never said. Maybe we could tell somebody, when we get the chance, and they could tell the Comanche agent."

Leo made a weary sound. "Poor John, he just never wanted to be a farmer. Well, he don't have to worry about that now."

Toward midnight they decided that they had traveled about as far as they could go without resting. When they got their breath they rolled John Coyotesong out of the saddle and began gathering rocks to build a burial mound. When they finished with the mound they stood for a few minutes in silence. "I wonder if John was a religious man?" Leo said at last.

"I don't think he ever said."

"Well, so long, John. When you get to where you're goin', I hope you like it better'n the place you come from." They got in their saddles and rode for another hour before finally stopping for the night.

Frank Beeler had just topped a rocky ridge and had stopped to let his roan blow when he heard the shot that killed John Coyotesong. It was no more than a faint "pop" in the late afternoon, a small bubble of sound bursting in the still air. He knew instinctively what had happened.

Well, he thought bleakly, they never was cut out to be outlaws anyhow. Sooner or later it had to happen. They would have done something foolish and a lawman or a posseman would have killed them, thinking they were as dangerous as their reputations claimed they were. Or some hard time bounty hunter would track them down and kill them for the money. It was all in the cards.

But goddamnit, Beeler thought with a sudden unexpected surge of anger, it didn't have to happen like this! Hunted down and shot for the pure sport of the thing!

Still, he reminded himself, it was none of his business. When he got to Arkansas he would tell some friends about the macabre hunting party, but he couldn't expect anything to be done about it. The murders would be impossible to prove. And the killing of outlaws was hardly to be considered murder in the first place. The Brannon bunch would simply disappear, and that would be the end of it. And Warren Conmy and Ben Sutter would go off somewhere looking for other entertainment.

The point is, Beeler told himself, it's none of my business.

Already he was reining his roan around and was heading back toward the sound of the shot.

It was well past dark when he reached the ridge where he had parted with the outlaws. There was no sign of the Brannons, no shallow graves, no burial mounds. Beeler couldn't believe that Conmy had missed his target a second time; a man of his enormous ego simply would not have allowed that to happen. No . . . he felt sure that at least one of the outlaws was dead. The live ones had taken the body with them.

He led the roan to higher ground, and there on a distant slope he saw the campfire stabbing in the darkness. There was something shocking in the arrogance of men who would coolly commit murder and then brazenly expose themselves to attack from the survivors. Probably, Beeler thought, they didn't think of the outlaws as men at all, but as "game," the same as bear or wolf. Who ever heard of a bear or wolf returning to stalk the hunter? It was unthinkable.

Beeler was sorely tempted to prove to them that the unthinkable could happen.

It was a pleasant thought, but he knew that it was only wishful dreaming. One revolver against three expert rifles could not work. What he had to do was find what was left of the Brannon bunch; together, maybe they could do something.

The fire had been Conmy's idea. He was in high spirits after killing the Indian and evening the score with Sutter. "I have a right," he insisted, "to a little celebration. Even if all we have to drink is coffee. Duane, you did think to bring coffee, didn't you?"

"There's some in the saddle roll," the secretary told him. "But do you think we ought to risk a fire?"

Conmy turned and said sarcastically, "That's exactly what I think."

Ben Sutter started to speak, but then changed his mind, shrugged, and helped Keating gather firewood. More and more he had been aware of these brief little clashes between Warren and Duane Keating, and they disturbed him. It's Verna, he thought in quiet anger at his sister. He knew very well that there could never be anything between Keating and his sister, but Verna persisted in those little things that she knew made her husband furious. The little smiles that she beamed in Keating's direction. The way she casually touched him. It was Verna's way of telling her husband that she was still displeased that he had hired Keating in the first place. It was uncomfortable having a former suitor nearby all the time, almost as one of the family. Not that she didn't like Keating, or love her husband completely—it simply wasn't comfortable having an old friend doing servant's work.

Later, as Keating was looking after the horses, Sutter said, "Maybe it would be a good thing to let up on Duane for a while."

Warren smiled innocently. "How do you mean?"

"You know how I mean. You've been cutting him down, like a butcher taking slices off a piece of sausage, ever since you and Verna were married."

"If Duane doesn't like working for me, he is free to quit."

Ben Sutter sighed to himself. He could see that this line of reasoning would get him nowhere. He looked into the fire and thought for several seconds. "There's another thing you might want to think about," he said slowly. "Accidents have been known to happen on hunting trips. If I were you, I'd be a little careful about the way I walked in front of Duane's rifle."

Conmy smiled. He knew exactly what Ben was getting at, and it didn't disturb him in the least. "You worry too much, Ben. It takes guts to kill a man. Keating doesn't have them."

"Killing a man is not such a big thing, as we both have reason to know."

Conmy laughed.

They took turns standing watch that night, with

Keating taking the hated middle watch, as always. He sat well away from the fire, his rifle across his knees. He was not a natural hunter like Warren and Ben, but he was alert and sensitive to all the subtle changes in the night. In the years that he had been on Warren Conmy's payroll, he had deliberately set out to master all the things in a man that Verna admired. He had learned to shoot and track expertly. Blindfolded, he could sort out the great vintages of red burgundy. He could tell in an instant whether a goose liver came from France or from Germany. He could stay in the saddle for days at a time, and he could kill quickly and cleanly, although he had never killed a man.

Suddenly, he found himself gazing coolly down the barrel of his rifle, the sights centered squarely on the form of Warren Conmy sleeping near the fire. An almost paralyzing thrill struck him when he realized what he was doing. It would be so easy simply to squeeze the trigger, and, like magic, there would be no more Warren Conmy.

Of course, it was not nearly that simple. Killing Warren would mean that he would also have to kill Ben. And, sooner or later, he would probably have to kill Humphrey O'Toole. And even if he should do all that, it would only gain him Verna's hatred, not her love.

He smiled ruefully and again rested the rifle on his knees. Nothing was ever simple when dealing with the Conmys and the Sutters.

Two hours before daybreak he woke Ben for the last watch. "Is everything quiet?"

"As the grave," Keating said.

"All right, get some rest. Tomorrow's apt to be a long day."

"Do you think you can finish up tomorrow?"

"There shouldn't be any trouble about that. There're only two of them left. They're not very smart, and they're rotten shots. Tell you the truth, this game is proving to be something of a disappointment to me; it was more fun hunting buffalo in Africa."

Keating smiled. That was going to be a great comfort to the Brannons, knowing that they were less amusing to kill than buffalo. He asked casually, "What if Beeler gets back in the game?"

"He won't. Beeler's no fool; he knows that staying with the outlaws would only get him killed." He shook his head. "No, Beeler's halfway to Arkansas by this time. I suppose he'll tell some wild story about two eastern dudes who came west to kill outlaws for sport, but nobody'll believe him. Even if they did, there's nothing they could do about it. The Brannons, after all, are wanted men."

Keating threw his bedroll by the fire, but sleep did not come quickly. It had been a heady experience simply looking at Warren over the sights of his rifle. It had started a thought growing in his mind. Warren Conmy was mortal; he could die like anybody else. Since their childhood days he had not been quite sure of that.

The next morning they rode across the wooded valley and up the far slope to where Conmy had shot the Indian. There was no body there, and this did nothing to soothe Warren's rising temper. Ben looked at him and smiled crookedly. "Are you sure you killed him?"

Conmy whirled on his brother-in-law. "Are you suggesting I'm lying?"

"I'm not suggesting anything, I'm just wondering where the body is."

"Maybe they took it with them. Maybe they buried it." With a visible effort he reined in his temper. "Well, it won't be long before we find out; they left a set of tracks behind that even Duane could follow."

Ben noticed that for once Keating did not respond to one of Warren's little jabs. He sat calmly with his hands folded on the saddle horn, saying nothing. Conmy didn't appear to notice anything unusual, but Ben couldn't help wondering at the source of the secretary's self-containment.

As it turned out it was Keating who found the burial mound, a simple oval of rocks piled up around the body to ward off attacks of coyotes and buzzards. "Tear it down," Conmy said to Keating.

Obediently, Keating removed the top layer of rocks. Conmy beamed happily at the sight of that brown dead face. "Look at that, right through the heart!" He laughed at Sutter. "I told you he was dead!"

Inspecting the ground, Keating said, "It looks like they struck north after burying the Indian. Do you think they could be headed back to the Creek Nation?"

Sutter scowled. "Why would they do that? They'd stand a much better chance here in the hills."

"Maybe they have friends among the Creeks."

"Then why did they pass them by in the first place?"

"I don't know," Conmy said, recovering from the confirmation of his kill. "But I've got a feeling we'd better start finding out."

From time to time they would lose the trail for short distances, and then pick it up again with little trouble. The outlaws seemed to be running in panic, paying little attention to their backtrail. Then, toward midafternoon they found the place where the Brannons had slept. They also found a third set of hoofmarks.

All three riders got down and studied the marks for some tine. At last Ben Sutter looked up and said, "Beeler. The hooves are unshod; it must be one of the animals taken from the drunk Choctaws. It all adds up to Beeler. He's decided to throw in with the outlaws after all."

CHAPTER EIGHT

Beeler was beginning to know the outlaws. He guessed that panic would have overtaken them by this time, and they would strike blindly to the north, blundering through brush and timber, giving no thought to the kind of trail they were leaving behind them. He also knew Conmy and Sutter as competent trackers as well as expert killers; they would pounce on the outlaws' trail as soon as it was light enough to see.

Beeler decided not to go through the slow business of tracking, but to take the most direct possible route to the north in the hope of overtaking the remainder of the Brannon bunch.

It worked. Shortly before noon he found the two brothers sitting on the ground dully chewing jerky while their jaded horses grazed nearby. Babe Brannon grabbed nervously for his rifle as Beeler approached. *Much too slow,* Beeler thought. If he had been Conmy or Sutter, they would have been dead.

The outlaw brothers got unsteadily to their feet, staring at the former lawman. "Mister," Leo told him, "you take some big chances. Don't you know you could get yourself shot ridin' up on a body that way?"

"If I'd been Conmy or Sutter you'd both be dead by this time." With some effort Beeler resisted the temptation to lecture them. He got down from the saddle and stretched his legs and rubbed his wounded shoulder. "I take it," he said, "that John Coyotesong is dead."

Babe and Leo nodded sadly. "Shot right out of the saddle, from a long ways off. Telescope. We buried him last night, back up the trail a piece."

Babe took a long, thoughtful look at Beeler and said, "We figgered you'd be most to Arkansas by this time. What made you change your mind?"

Beeler grinned sourly. "I remember tellin' John that he had a favor comin' from me. I guess it's time he got it—even if it's too late to do him any good."

They recrossed the Canadian shortly before sundown and made dry camp on a wooded hill overlooking the river. "Tomorrow," Beeler told his two partners, "we'll talk to Hooker. With luck he'll take us in and keep us out of sight until Conmy and Sutter decide to take up another brand of sport."

"Somehow," Leo complained, "it rubs me the wrong way to have to hide out from that pair of murderin' dudes. I'd almost be happier if they was marshals." He looked at Beeler. "You used to be a lawman, ain't there anything can be done about them?"

"Not as long as they stick to killin' wanted outlaws." He gazed into space for a moment. A queer, cold sensation settled in his guts. Somehow, in spite of all that had happened, he had, until this moment, thought of himself as immune to Conmy's and Sutter's murderous little whims. Because he was a former lawman. Because he did *not* have a price on his head. And because he was *not* an outlaw. Now things had changed. He was, in a strictly legal way, an outlaw. He was a horse thief. He had also given aid and comfort to known outlaws, which branded him with the same iron. All of which, in the eyes of Conmy and Sutter, made him fair game.

"Get back in your saddles," he told the brothers. "We got us some ridin' to do."

For the best part of the afternoon Beeler led them along a corkscrew trail, over rockbeds, and through swift-running little streams. He cut brush and dragged it at the end of his rope to erase hoofprints on soft earth. From time to time they would split up, laying down false trails. At the end of the day Beeler was reasonably sure that Conmy and Sutter were no longer finding tracking the easy work that it had been earlier.

"How far are we from that meetin' house?" Leo Brannon asked wearily.

"Not far, but we'll stop pretty soon and go the rest of the way in the mornin'. Some of the old Creeks are skittish about white folks and their way of doin' things; I'd just as soon not ride up on them in the dark."

They rode until the sun had settled behind the

dark timber and then made camp in a grove of cottonwoods, along with a flock of turkeys.

"How well do you know this Indian preacher?" Babe asked as they settled down for the night.

"I did him a favor once—I guess he'll remember."

They passed the night in chill discomfort and with grumbling bellies. Above their heads the big birds clucked and gobbled and moved about on cottonwood limbs, but no foreign sound disturbed the silence of those dark hills. "I think we lost them," Beeler said to no one in particular.

Wrapped in his blanket, he stared up at the gunmetal sky. The past few days lay somewhere behind a curtain of unreality; he could almost believe that his meeting with Sutter and Conmy had never taken place. The whole adventure was too bizarre—the peg-legged butler, the dead-shot secretary, the two carefree young men who murdered for sport, and the beautiful Mrs. Conmy who saw nothing wrong with any of it. Beeler could almost believe that none of it had happened.

Then he rolled over on his wounded shoulder and the pain caused him to wince. He could believe it.

It was still dark when the blood-chilling howl jarred them awake. The two outlaws jumped to their feet in alarm. "Godamighty!" Leo gasped. "What *was* that?"

"Ain't like nothin' I ever heard before!" Babe muttered, sweeping the darkness with his rifle.

They heard it again, a deep-throated blaring, like a lost soul crying in the night. "Beeler, where are you? What the hell *is* that noise?"

Beeler sat up on his blanket, startled as the sound echoed and re-echoed in the timber. It sounded a third time, then a fourth. At last Beeler began to grin. "Settle down, boys, it's just the *pufketa*."

"The *what?*"

"The deacon's horn. The Creeks use it to call the congregation together."

"At *this* time of the night?"

"It must be close to dawn. Sunup is when the Creeks commence their church services." Hooker had explained it to him once. Christ had said, "Look for me early in the morning." And that is what they did.

Beeler threw off his blanket and stood up and stretched. "If anybody's been wonderin' what day of the week it is, now we know. It's Sunday. That means that Hooker's goin' to be busy the best part of the day; we'll have to watch our chances to catch him."

As the first light of dawn touched the glossy cottonwood leaves, the *pufketa* sounded four more long blasts. "The service is ready to commence," Beeler told the two outlaws. "We won't get to see Hooker before dinnertime, but it wouldn't hurt to move up a little closer."

As they led their horses through the timber they could hear the singing in the meeting house. The words were Creek and the voices were unbelievably sad and sweet. As they neared the large clearing that served as churchyard and campground they heard Brother Hooker's deep, forceful voice beginning a long and powerful prayer.

In the center of the clearing was the church itself—the *Mekko Sapkv Coko*, House of Prayer. It was a long, shotgun-style frame building, perfectly plain, sporting no sign of a steeple or cross. Surrounding the church were a dozen or more camp houses, each complete with its own hitching ground, water well, and privy.

"Looks more like a town than a church," Leo said, cocking his head and scowling.

"The Creeks take their religion serious," Beeler told him. "Most of them travel all day to get here, some of them walk. Once they get here they expect the preachin' to last all day Sunday, and sometimes Monday as well. That's what the camp houses are for."

Babe Brannon shook his head in wonder. "Our old ma was a churchgoin' woman herself—but not like this." He nodded toward the church house. "Is that Brother Hooker talkin' now?"

"No." A quieter, sterner voice was speaking now. The words were Creek, but Beeler could make out most of them. "It's the parson, I think.

Gettin' ready to take up a collection for the family of somebody that's died." He listened for a while longer, then turned to the two outlaws and groaned. "There's goin' to be a funeral."

"Stands to reason"—Leo shrugged—"if a body's dead."

"A Creek funeral lasts four days, sometimes longer. That means that Hooker's not goin' to have much time for us."

"When's the funeral start?"

"I can't tell. Tomorrow most likely; maybe Tuesday."

Leo shrugged again. It seemed like a small matter.

Babe said, "When're you goin' to talk to this preacher?"

"At dinnertime, with a little luck. They'll knock off for maybe an hour while the womenfolks fix somethin' to eat."

They unbitted and staked their horses in the trees. As they waited for noon they listened to several different voices discussing what seemed to be church business. Then there was another spell of singing followed by an overwhelming two-hour sermon from Brother Hooker. When the congregation came outside for the midday meal they looked slightly stunned by the length and power of the preaching.

A tall, gray ramrod of a man appeared at the church door, shaking hands with members of the congregation as they left the building. Beeler sighed to himself when he saw him. It had been almost three years since they had met—he had almost forgotten what an imposing person the preacher actually was.

Women in long gray dresses and overall aprons, their heads wrapped in bright-colored scarves, headed directly for the camp houses. Within a few minutes the air was fragrant with woodsmoke and cooking food. The menfolks, most of them wearing shapeless black suits and looking like dirt farmers everywhere, stood in little clusters in front of the meeting house. They talked quietly of the weather, crops, the power of the preaching. The deacons, seven of them, strolled around the grounds with great dignity, holding firmly to their beautifully carved staves and looking a little—Beeler thought—like Moses must have looked on that fateful day on Sinai.

The parson, the spiritual leader of the church, stood talking to Brother Duel Hooker, while a young licensed minister and two visiting preachers stood listening in respectful silence. Beeler waited impatiently until an imposing-looking old woman—probably a class leader—came up and took the parson's arm and led him away.

"All right," Beeler told his two partners, "I'll see what I can do."

He walked out of the timber and started across

the sprawling churchyard. With no show of surprise, a few of the men nodded to him as he made his way toward the church. "Howdy, Mr. Working," Beeler said gravely. "How are you, Mr. Colton?" Like most deputy marshals, he had made it a point to know the influential Indians in the District when he had been riding for the court. A few of the men nodded solemnly and said, "Marshal." Most of them merely looked; experience had taught them that rarely was the appearance of a white man in their midst a cause for rejoicing.

Brother Hooker broke off what he had been saying to the two visiting preachers. With uncharacteristic abruptness, he nodded and then turned to meet Beeler. The two men met in front of the church and stood for a moment smiling. "Well," the preacher said at last, "I wonder what brings a man of the law to the house of God?"

His smile, Beeler noted, was rather strained and singularly lacking in warmth. Hooker knew that at long last all debts were being called in, as he had known some day they would. He visibly braced himself to pay whatever was demanded. "I'm not a marshal any more," Beeler told him casually. "But you might be in a way to do me a favor, if you're a mind to."

"You know I'll do whatever I can, Marshal. I have not forgotten that I am in your debt."

It was not going as well as Beeler had hoped. "Is

there some place we can talk? Some place a little more private than this?"

The preacher thought for a moment. "There's the Waterman camp house. There's no one there today." They circled the church and walked casually toward one of the smaller camp houses near the edge of the clearing. As they walked they talked quietly of matters in which they had no interest at all. From the side of his eye, Beeler studied the tall Indian and wondered if he had made a mistake in coming here. Hooker was a new breed of preacher; he had been well educated in Baptist schools and spoke English better than most of the white intruders in the Territory. On rare occasions he even preached in English—to the displeasure of his congregation—but at the core he was all Creek and he knew too well that no Indian ever got the best of it when dealing with a white man.

But Brother Duel Hooker owed Frank Beeler for the life of his only son. For years he had waited, often in fear, for the marshal to demand his own brand of payment. He knew now the time had come.

The Waterman camp house was furnished with a small cookstove, two wall bunks, a plank table, and two cane-bottom chairs. The two men sat at the table and looked at each other in silence. Beeler said, "Is Tom all right now?"

"Tom is well," the preacher said tonelessly. "He is with friends in the Chickasaw Nation."

Beeler realized too late that it was a mistake to start off with mention of the preacher's son—it was too much like collecting an honorable debt at the point of a gun. "I'm glad he's all right," he said lamely. And that, for the moment, concluded the subject of young Tom Hooker. He spread his hands on the table and asked, "Brother Hooker, have you ever heard of a gang of outlaws called the Brannon bunch?"

The Indian's eyes widened. "Of course. They are murderers and robbers. Very bad men."

Beeler smiled wryly. "Not exactly. Up until a few days ago they were a bunch of farm boys tryin' to make ends meet by holdin' up banks and trains." For several minutes he sketched the disastrous career of Leo and Babe Brannon and their followers. Then he tried to describe Warren Conmy and Ben Sutter and the savage little pastime that they had invented. But the longer he talked, the clearer it became that the preacher did not believe a word of it.

At last Hooker raised his hand like some biblical prophet and said, "Please, Marshal, there is no need to go on. I understand that you are in trouble and that you have come to me for help. Very well, if it is in my power I will help you."

"But you don't believe my story about the Brannons."

"It does not matter what I believe. I owe you for the life of my son. I will help you in any way I can."

"Well," Beeler said reluctantly, "I'd rest easier if you'd believe some of what I told you about Conmy and Sutter, if not the Brannons. But I guess it's not important." He thought for a minute. "I've got the Brannon brothers with me. They're hidin' in the timber south of the clearin'. What I want you to do is put them up for a spell—two, three weeks maybe."

Brother Duel Hooker looked appalled. "Are you asking me to invite murderers into the *Mekko Sapkv Coko*?"

"No, but I'd be much obliged if you'd let them stay here in the camp house until you can get them to your own place later on."

"This camp house is on churchground; it is God's place."

Beeler regarded him with sudden coldness. "All right. If you don't want to help. I had thought maybe you would." He shoved himself up from the table and started for the door. "Would it be askin' too much," he said acidly, "if I asked you to be quiet about this visit? Especially if a pair of eastern dudes by the name of Conmy and Sutter come askin'?"

Hooker's brown face had gone quietly gray. He slumped over the table and slowly nodded. "All right," he said huskily. "After dinner, when preaching starts again, bring the outlaws here. After services tonight, if it's possible, I'll take them to my house with me."

"Thank you." Beeler was tempted to try once more to explain about Conmy and Sutter, but in the end he decided against it. How could he expect the preacher to believe a story so bizarre that he could hardly believe it himself? "I'm sorry," he said wearily. "I don't want you to do anything against your will."

The preacher merely looked at him, and after a moment he got up from the table and walked out of the camp house.

Several minutes later a young woman appeared at the door and handed Beeler a large bowl of sofkee and blue dumplings. A gift, she said in Creek, to the white marshal from the camp house of John Forestman. Beeler dimly remembered Forestman as a small rancher whose stock he had once rescued from rustlers. "Thank you," he said in her own language. "And thanks to your father and to the women of your camp house."

The young woman dropped her head sadly, and Beeler saw that her eyes were red from weeping. The Forestman family was greatly honored, she said, that the marshal had troubled himself to come here in this time of her family's grief.

At first Beeler didn't understand. Then he did. It was the young woman's brother, Jack Forestman, for whom funeral services were being held the next day.

Shortly after Beeler accepted the food from the Forestman woman, a deacon appeared in front of the church with a great curved horn—taken long ago from some Texas longhorn steer—and sounded his four nerve-shattering calls. Quickly all members of the congregation cleared their tables, finished with the dinner dishes, and hurried back to the church. Once again the air was filled with the strange, sweet sound of Creek singing. Beeler left the camp house and headed for the timber where he had left the Brannon brothers.

"What in damnation are they doin' now?" Leo demanded. "Don't these folks do nothin' but sing and pray and listen to preachin'?"

"They eat," Beeler told him dryly. "There's some grub at the camp house that will hold you over till tonight."

"Has the preacher agreed to hide us out?"

"Yes. For a little while, anyway. After preachin's over tonight he'll take us to his house on Possum Creek." Beeler regarded them sourly. "I can't say that he's right happy about it, but he'll do it."

"What have you got on that Indian anyhow," Babe wanted to know, "to make him take in a pair of white folks like us?"

"It was a long time ago." Beeler shrugged. "It doesn't matter now."

But it did matter, and the Brannons had a right to some sort of explanation. "It was a white intruder, by the name of McRill," Beeler told them. "He took a fancy to young Tom Hooker's wife. One night when Tom was away McRill broke into the house and . . ." He looked at them. "Well, when Tom came home and found out what had happened, he took his gun and went after McRill and killed him. McRill bein' a white man, that made it a case for the federal court, and I was the deputy in this part of the Territory at the time." He smiled faintly. "It was my fault, I guess. I let Tom get away from me, and I never did find him. Somehow Preacher Hooker figgered I did it on purpose."

The outlaws regarded him narrowly, not sure that they could trust a lawman who had taken an Indian's part against a white man. "Well," Leo said at last, "I guess this McRill, everything considered, wasn't much account anyhow."

"That's a fact," Beeler told them with the same faint smile. "He wasn't." And that ended the subject of Tom Hooker.

They staked their horses and crossed the churchyard as quickly and quietly as possible. Inside the Waterman camp house, Babe Brannon looked doubtfully at the corn sofkee and blue dumplings. "I never seen any grub that looked like *this* before."

"It's the only food you're likely to see for a while, so you'd better start gettin' used to it," Beeler told them. They found some spoons in a storage box beside the stove and dug into the strange-tasting food. From the church, Brother Hooker's voice rolled powerfully across the clearing. Absently they picked their teeth and listened to the long stretches of praying and preaching, interrupted at infrequent intervals with a hymn from the Creek songbook.

Leo sat heavily at the table and sighed. “Boys, it’s goin’ to be a long day!”

And it was.

Shortly before sundown one of the visiting preachers wound up with a long and unbelievably monotonous prayer, and the congregation filed out for supper. Once again fires were built in cookstoves, coffee was put on to boil, the smell of food perfumed the air. The men went to see about their teams, the women who weren’t cooking gossiped in small clusters in front of the camp houses.

“Don’t these people ever go home?” Leo asked wearily.

“When preachin’s over,” Beeler told him. Which, he knew, wouldn’t be until after midnight, if then. But he didn’t tell them that.

After a while, another woman from the Forestman camp house brought them a large bowl of sofkee and another of grape dumplings. As they were eating, Brother Duel Hooker appeared in the doorway. The preacher regarded the two outlaws with dark disapproval. Then he turned to Beeler. “I have spoken to my wife; you and your friends will be welcome at our house. But not until the day after tomorrow.”

Beeler stiffened. “Why is that?”

"The funeral tomorrow. The body has lain at the Forestman house for two days; the family is bringing it to the church directly after services tonight." He looked coolly and directly at Beeler. "You will attend all funeral services, of course."

"I'm sorry, Preacher, I don't think I ought to do that."

"You must," Hooker said in a tone that left no leeway for argument. "The family expects it. All who knew young Jack Forestman when he was alive are expected to attend his funeral. Failing to do so would be an unforgivable insult to the Forestmans." A very small and stony smile glinted for a moment in those dark eyes. "You had better ask yourself one question, Marshal. Is your position so strong at this moment that you can afford to insult one of the Creek Nation's most influential families?"

Beeler said ruefully, "I'll attend the funeral. What about my friends?"

"They may remain in the camp house, if they wish."

"Ain't there some way we can get away before the end of the funeral?" He didn't like the idea of being at the center of so much attention. A Creek funeral was an important event; it was the kind of thing that Conroy and Sutter would be naturally attracted to.

But the preacher shook his head. "Until the time of burial the bereaved family is in complete control of the church. The Forestmans have directed the parson to begin the funeral services at midnight, out of consideration of their many friends. Otherwise the congregation would have to wait for another day or more on the churchgrounds, much to the inconvenience of all concerned."

"What was *that* all about?" Leo demanded when the preacher had returned to the church.

"The Forestmans expect me to attend the funeral, and I have to do it, or they will be insulted. And we don't want that."

"Why not? Who are the Forestmans?"

"For one thing, a Forestman is captain of the Creek Light Horse Police."

The outlaw slumped resignedly. "Go to the funeral."

On the afternoon of their second day from camp, Conmy and Sutter lost the outlaws' trail completely. It led to a bed of shale, then to a rock-bottom stream and disappeared. All they were sure of was that the Brannons, and Beeler, had been headed generally north.

"Why?" Conmy demanded angrily. "Why would they leave the comparative safety of the hills?"

Sutter slouched wearily in the saddle. "I don't know. But Beeler's got something in mind, and I don't think I'm going to like it."

"What do you mean?"

"We could make more trouble for ourselves than

we're able to handle. Killing a former United States marshal is not the same as killing one of the Brannon gang."

"If the idea scares you, you're free to return to camp."

"It doesn't scare me, I just don't see much sense to it any more. As things stand, the game's a draw. Why can't we break it off and try something else?"

"Because," Warren answered coldly, "this is the game we're playing, and I don't intend to leave it unfinished." He raised his hand and snapped his fingers impatiently. "Duane, bring that canteen up here."

Keating kneed up to Conmy's elbow and handed him the saddle canteen. "Maybe Ben's right," he said quietly. "Why not move on to something else?"

Conmy turned on him. "When I want a secretary's advice, I'll ask for it."

Ben Sutter regarded the paleness of Keating's face and shifted uneasily in the saddle. "Duane, would you mind riding up ahead and seeing where this trail leads to?"

As Keating spurred stiffly ahead, Ben looked at his brother-in-law with disapproval. "You're asking for trouble, Warren."

"From Duane?" Conmy laughed. "Don't be a fool."

"Don't you forget what I said about getting in

front of his rifle. Well . . ." He shrugged. "At least we ought to return to camp and let Verna and Hump know what's happened to us. Hot food in our stomachs and a little rest; tomorrow we can move the camp to the north bank of the Canadian."

Warren, in spite of his determination and anger, felt himself sag with weariness. His injured leg was throbbing, and the prospect of hot food and a night's sleep was irresistible.

The next day they moved their camp to the north bank of the Canadian, and that afternoon they saw their first family of Creek farmers headed toward the Three Forks area. Warren waved the wagon down and said, "We're looking for three men—white men—who were headed in this direction yesterday. We'd be willing to pay five dollars to the man who helps us find them."

The Indians looked at them with cool dark eyes and shrugged. The man driving the wagon said something in Creek, then pointed to his mouth and shook his head.

"They don't speak English," Ben Sutter said.

"Maybe," Warren said grimly, "but I don't think so." Suddenly he grabbed the stock of his Marlin and snapped the weapon out of the saddle boot. He pointed it at the chest of the wide-eyed Indian. "You do speak English, don't you, mister?"

The man stared anxiously at the muzzle of the rifle.

"Hard luck for you if you don't," Warren told the man with a savage grin.

Alarmed, Ben grabbed his brother-in-law's arm. "For God's sake, he doesn't speak English! That's all there is to it!"

"He's lying," Conmy said coldly. "Watch this." He shook free of Ben's hand and tightened the grip of the rifle. His finger slowly started to squeeze the trigger. "It's up to you, mister. Are you going to start answering my questions, or do I shoot?"

The Indian's brown face glistened with sweat. His wife grabbed his arm and shook him excitedly. "What do you want?" he asked Conmy, shoving his wife away.

Conmy laughed explosively. "See?" he said to Ben. "I told you he was lying. All right," he told the Creek, "now that you've learned to speak English, I want to know about the three white men. They're outlaws; it'll mean trouble to you if you protect them."

"No white man." The Indian shook his head several times. His wife stared fearfully at the rifle that Conmy still aimed at the Indian's chest.

"Where are you going?" Ben asked.

The Creek pointed to some loose boards and carpenter's tools in the back of the wagon. "Indian boy dead. Funeral. Build gravehouse."

Sutter turned to Conmy again. "He hasn't seen Beeler or the Brannons. Let him go."

"The man's a liar," Conmy told him angrily. "What I ought to do is shoot him."

Cautiously, Ben kneed his animal against his brother-in-law's sorrel and moved the rifle barrel to one side. "It's all right," he told the Creek. "You can go now."

As the wagon disappeared into a stand of live oak, Ben turned to Warren Conmy and hissed angrily, "What the hell's wrong with you? This is Indian country; it *belongs* to them! You can't threaten to shoot people just because they don't happen to answer to suit you."

"If it should please me to shoot one of them," Conmy told him calmly, "that's what I'll do. Ben, I'm beginning to think you are losing your nerve."

Sutter stared at him for a moment. The rush of anger was hot in his face.

Warren smiled widely and slapped his brother-in-law on the back. "Forget what I just said. I knew all the time you weren't losing your nerve."

CHAPTER NINE

After supper the congregation gathered in the church for the third time that day. In the camp house Beeler and the Brannons could hear most of what was going on; the singing, the preaching, the praying. "Lord," Leo Brannon groaned to no one in particular, "I never seen such a bunch of folks for churchgoin'!"

At midnight the congregation filed into the dark churchyard and stood quietly for several minutes. At last a wagon belonging to the Forestman family entered the clearing from the east. It was followed by four more wagons bearing friends and relatives who had been sitting with the body for the past two days. The Forestmans at the camp house joined the funeral wagon and followed it on foot to the church. There the parson, an ancient, wise, and gentle man, met the bereaved parents and offered quiet words of comfort. At last the appointed pallbearers lowered the oak casket from the wagon, and flanked by deacons and class leaders, took the body into the church.

"I never seen a funeral at this time of night before," Babe Brannon said from the camp house doorway.

"The funeral won't be till day after tomorrow," Beeler told him. "Tonight friends of the Forestmans will sit with the body in the church.

Tomorrow there will be prayers and maybe services, depending on how the Forestmans feel about it. Then the next day, the funeral."

Leo Brannon sighed resignedly. "A lot of rigmarole, if you was to ask me. But I guess a body's got a right to plant his kinfolks any way that suits him."

Babe Brannon was sitting on the doorstep in front of the camp house. His belly was pleasantly filled with Indian food and he was reasonably content with the world. "Well," he said, "one thing about it, we're safe as long as the funeral holds out. There ain't *no*body skunk enough to bust up a funeral."

"You don't know Warren Conmy and Ben Sutter," Beeler thought to himself. But he didn't say it. He had enough to think about without getting the Brannon brothers nervous all over again.

The next morning, shortly before sunup, the deacon with the great steerhorn trumpet came to the front of the church and sounded his four shattering blasts to the congregation. All friends of the Forestmans, Frank Beeler among them, gathered inside the church to pray for the dead boy's soul. Beeler took a bench at the rear, on the left side of the church, in the place reserved for male visitors. The right side was the women's side.

The first light of the new day slanted through the open doorway and fell across the simple oak casket. All Creek churches faced the east, for it was believed that *Hesaketumese*, the Christ, when he returned to earth would come from the east with the sunrise.

The service lasted no more than an hour. There were brief subdued prayers from the parson, the preacher, a few of the elders. Then the congregation sang the eerily sweet "Illka Este?" (Where Shall the Body Rest?) and quietly filed out into the morning silent and moist with dew.

Beeler shook hands with John Forestman, and for a little while they talked about the dead boy, Jack, and about the cattle that Beeler had once saved from rustlers.

"How many more services today?" Leo asked when Beeler returned to the camp house.

"That's up to the dead boy's family. When they feel some prayers ought to be said, they'll let the horn deacon know, and he'll call the congregation."

There was another brief prayer service shortly before dinner. And a third service at midafternoon. In the meantime wagons filled with friends of the Forestmans were arriving from all over the Nation. By noontime the *Mekko Sapkv Coko* was not large enough to hold the many members of the Forestman family and their friends. During services the overflow stood just outside the door, but Beeler continued to occupy his bench in the rear of the church. He was, after all, a former

United States deputy marshal and a friend of the Forestmans. It was directly after the midafternoon service that day that Beeler saw Conmy and Sutter.

He had just stepped out of the church and was quietly making his way through the mourners on the outside—and there they were, coming directly toward him. They were strolling casually across the clearing, swinging their rifles carelessly as they took in the bustle and spectacle of the Creek funeral.

Beeler froze. There was nowhere to run, nowhere to hide. His hand went instinctively to the place where his revolver should have been—but mourners at a funeral did not go armed. Not, anyway, at a Creek funeral.

Several of the Indians had seen the two white men, but they were not alarmed or even very interested. White men seemed to have the notion that they were free to go where they pleased, do as they pleased, especially in Indian Territory. Most of the Indians were tolerant, so long as they did not slaughter too much of the game or molest the women.

But to come armed in a churchyard, to a funeral—not all of them were so tolerant about this. A very tall, broad-shouldered Creek appeared at Beeler's side and asked quietly, "Trouble?"

Beeler looked up at him and made himself smile. "I don't think so."

"Friends of yours?" the Indian asked.

"I know them." There was no time to explain Conmy and Sutter to the big Creek; and anyway he wouldn't have understood. On top of that, there was almost nothing an Indian could do about white intruders except report them to federal authorities. "They're green," he added, "and don't know the customs here. All the same, it might be best if we talked to them together."

That was when Conmy and Sutter saw him. Conmy's face went pale. He grabbed his rifle in both hands, but Sutter quickly turned his head and spoke sharply, and the rifle was not raised to firing position.

Beeler had been holding himself so rigid that his shoulders and back began to ache. Now he relaxed. The first fateful moment had passed, and without shooting. There was still a chance that something might be done, a tentative peace worked out, at least for the duration of the funeral.

If the big Creek had noticed the quick, almost silent scene between the two young sportsmen, his dark face did not show it. "There," he said to Beeler, "is another one."

It was Keating, lounging casually on the edge of the clearing, but alert and watchful, his rifle cradled conveniently in the crook of his arm. "Never mind about him now," Beeler said. "Let's talk to the others." They walked casually toward the center of the churchyard where Conmy and Sutter were standing.

Conmy had fully recovered from his first violent instinct to kill Beeler on the spot. He and Sutter were now perfectly at ease. They smiled as Beeler pulled up in front of them.

"Well," Conmy said pleasantly, "this *is* a bit of luck, Beeler. For a while we were afraid we'd lost you." With a perfectly natural and lively curiosity, he gazed out at the clusters of Creek mourners. "What's going on here anyway?"

"A funeral." Beeler was faintly surprised to hear his words come out naturally and quietly.

"Is it about over?" Conmy asked.

"No, it won't be over until tomorrow sometime."

Conmy gazed up at the summer sky and scratched the point of his jaw and seemed to sigh. "Too bad. I don't think I want to wait that long."

Beeler said nothing to that. The big Creek folded his arms across his broad chest and regarded the whites with curiosity, but he did not speak. At last Ben Sutter looked at Beeler and asked, "Does your friend speak English?"

Beeler allowed himself a tight smile. "Gentlemen," he said dryly, "meet Captain George Forestman of the Creek Light Horse Police. Captain, meet Mr. Conmy and Mr. Sutter."

The two men blinked and stared for a moment at the big Indian. Then Conmy laughed. "Beeler, you're full of surprises, I'll give you that much. But you haven't answered Ben's question. Does he speak English?"

"Some. When he takes the notion."

"I know," Conmy said, nodding his head. "I met another Indian like that not long ago."

Captain Forestman quickly cocked his head to one side and regarded the white men with new interest. Only that morning John River and his wife, old friends of the Forestman family, had told the captain about two white men who had stopped them on their way to the funeral and threatened them with rifles while demanding information about two white outlaws. John River had taken them for bounty hunters.

Conmy again scratched his chin and looked thoughtfully at the summer sky. Then he and Sutter looked at each other, and Beeler could almost hear their minds mesh and become as one. In some strange, silent way they had evaluated the changing situation and had made a decision. "Captain," Sutter said to George Forestman, "would you mind if we talked to Mr. Beeler alone for a minute?"

The Creek looked at Beeler, and Beeler nodded. "Well," Conmy smiled when the Light Horseman had moved away, "like I said, Beeler, you're full of surprises. You're also very lucky. In spite of all the trouble you've put us to, we're going to give you another chance to get out of this alive. Where are the Brannons?"

Beeler almost laughed; such enormous gall had to be admired. Here they were surrounded by two hundred Indians, including a captain of Light Horse, and none of them exactly friendly, but they managed somehow to ignore it all. They were, after all, the Conmys and the Sutters. Nothing could happen to them.

"We know the outlaws are with you," Ben said. "We tracked you from north of the Sans Bois almost to the Canadian. You and the Brannons." He looked curiously at the church, then at the scattered camp houses. "Where are they? In the church? In one of those camp shacks? Maybe even hiding under a tarp in one of the wagons?"

Conmy shrugged. "It doesn't matter. When the funeral's over and the Indians go home, we'll find them."

"We'll go through every Indian wagon, if we have to," Ben said, idly polishing the stock of his Marlin.

"And don't tell us we can't get away with it," Conmy added. "Do you think these Indians are going to protect a pair of white outlaws and risk getting themselves in trouble with federal courts? Don't be a fool, Beeler."

"Lucky," Ben said, returning to an earlier thought of Conmy's. "There's no other explanation for you, Beeler. In spite of all the trouble you've been to us, we're going to let you go. You don't even have to tell us where the Brannons are hiding; we'll take care of that ourselves. All you've got to do is walk away . . . alive."

Conmy grinned widely. "It's the best offer you'll ever get, Beeler."

Beeler was inclined to agree. He knew that the Indians were not going to risk enraging a federal court because of two white outlaws. His only protection here was the fragile sponsorship of Brother Duel Hooker, and that would not last long if the mood of the congregation turned against them.

"What about it?" Ben asked indifferently, still polishing the Marlin's stock. "Once we offered you money, and you refused it. Now we offer you your life. Just walk away and don't give us any more trouble."

"A funeral," Conmy smiled. "There's something poetic there. It could be your funeral too, Beeler. Think about it."

He did think about it, and he found the proposition tempting. But there was more to it than just a chance to save his own life. He had a genuine liking and respect for the bereaved Forestmans. The thought of starting a war in the middle of a funeral was obscene to him.

Conmy said, "There's Keating over there by the edge of the clearing—he's more dangerous than he looks; he's a dead shot. And back there somewhere out of sight is Hump—I think you already have some reason to respect Hump's marksmanship. So you see, Beeler, we are going to get the Brannons one way or another. And maybe you as well. It's up to you."

The smart general, Beeler told himself, knew when to pull back and fight again some other day. But at that moment he wasn't feeling smart. Maybe it was because Conmy was bearing down too hard on his already battered pride. It might even have had something to do with the promise that he had made to the dead John Coyotesong. He shrugged resignedly and said, "I'll give you some free advice. Don't stand around the churchyard much longer with those rifles in your hands; George Forestman won't like it." Then he turned and walked away.

Conmy and Sutter watched him mingle with the other mourners. "I've known all along," Conmy said with a sigh, "but now I'm more sure of it than ever. We should have killed him long ago."

"Let him think on it for a while," Ben said. "He's not a fool; he could still change his mind."

"With night coming on, he and the Brannons could slip through our fingers in the darkness."

Ben shook his head. "We won't allow that to happen again."

They turned and strolled back to the edge of the clearing where Keating was waiting. "You and Hump keep an eye on Beeler," Conmy told the secretary. "If he goes to one of those camp houses or starts to leave the churchyard, I want to know about it immediately."

Verna Conmy was sitting on a campstool in front of her tent placidly watching a red squirrel race up and down a live-oak trunk. "I do wish you and Ben would drop this silly game," she told her husband with just a trace of pique. "Couldn't you do it this once, just for me?"

Warren Conmy dismounted and kissed his wife in an offhand way. "It's almost over," he assured her. "Hump and Duane are keeping an eye on things; the Brannons can't get away. The only thing I don't like is leaving you alone like this. You're all right, aren't you?"

"I'm bored," she told him coolly. "With not even Hump to talk to, just squirrels. How long do you expect this foolishness to go on?"

"We may end it later today. More likely tomorrow sometime."

"I wish you'd let it drop," she said again with an extravagant sigh.

Sutter, who had been watering the horses at the river, came up in time to hear part of his sister's complaint. "You can't blame her for being restless," he told Conmy. "With nobody to talk to, as she says, but the squirrels. Verna," he said, grinning suddenly, "how would you like to attend a Creek funeral?"

She sat erect, her eyes bright and lively. "Do you mean it?"

"Sure. The Indians won't mind; most likely they'll take it as an honor having a white woman in their church. It'll be something to tell your pals about when we get back to Chicago." He looked at his brother-in-law. "Don't you think so, Warren?"

Conmy regarded his beautiful wife and slowly began to grin. "I don't know why not. It would make them sit up and wonder, all right, a white woman suddenly appearing in the middle of things."

Verna suddenly laughed and clapped her hands, like a small girl who had just been promised a day at the circus.

As the horn deacon sounded the call for late afternoon prayer, Conmy and Sutter and Verna appeared out of the timber and started across the churchyard. A hush settled on the mourners who were filling the church. They regarded the trio with cool, dark eyes, neither pleased nor displeased. Earlier that day they had seen Captain Forestman talking to Beeler and the two young men; most of them assumed that the white men were friends of the Forestman family.

All the same, some of the Creeks regarded the whites with suspicion, if not hostility. They gave way, but grudgingly, as Verna and her escort approached the church. From the side of his mouth Conmy said, "I think it's just as well that we took Beeler's advice and left our rifles back at camp."

Sutter smiled faintly.

The deacon-usher appeared in the doorway and for just a moment betrayed surprise at seeing the three whites coming toward him. But he recovered quickly and, gesturing with his crooked staff, welcomed them into the *Mekko Sapkv Coko*.

Frank Beeler, in his usual place on the male visitors side of the church, was startled to see the three of them walking with supreme confidence, wide-eyed and faintly smiling, into the house of God, as if it were a music hall. The deacon indicated with his staff that Verna was to sit on the right-hand side of the church, the women's side, on a bench opposite Beeler's. Conmy and Sutter were directed to the left-hand side. They quickly, smilingly took their places on the bench, Conmy on Beeler's right, Sutter on his left.

After the brief, unsettled rustle that accompanied the entrance of the white visitors, the frail old parson took the pulpit and murmured a few words to the Forestman family which occupied the front benches. The casket, its lid covered with summer flowers, rested on a table in front of the pulpit. One of the Forestman women sobbed quietly as the old parson spoke.

Grinning, Conmy nudged Beeler with his elbow. "What's the old man talking about?"

Beeler shot him a look of cold anger, and Conmy raised his eyebrows and shrugged. For the duration of the service Beeler tried to ignore them, pretend they were not there. It was not easy.

The old parson took his seat alongside Brother Hooker, behind the pulpit, while a visiting preacher said a prayer. Sitting alone on the bench reserved for women visitors, Verna Conmy was listening to every strange guttural word with rapt attention. Rarely was a word of English heard inside the *Mekko Sapkv Coko*; the songbooks, the prayer books, and Bibles were all in Creek. None of this seemed to matter to Verna; she sat there with a delighted little smile at the corners of her mouth. From time to time she would glance across the aisle at her husband and laugh silently.

The congregation rose and sang the haunting hymn for the dead, "Illka Este?" after which Brother Duel Hooker delivered what was, for him, a brief and subdued prayer.

Through it all Conmy and Sutter sat back and observed with apparent delight. Beeler could almost see them making mental notes for the stories they would tell to their friends in Chicago. The amusing Indian funeral that they had witnessed. The funny little old parson, the deacons with their carved staves, the impossible language, and the strange music. Never mind the former

United States marshal who sat between them and whom they later intended to kill.

With the finish of Brother Hooker's prayer the congregation began to file out of the church. But Conmy and Sutter remained where they were, flanking Beeler. Sutter said in his absent but pleasant way, "I don't suppose you want to tell us about the Brannons, do you?"

"You must be crazy," Beeler snarled under his breath. "Do you think these people don't have feelings? Do you think you can just bust into a Creek funeral like it was a circus . . . ?"

"What the Indians think," Conmy said quietly, "is not important. Tomorrow we'll be gone, and that's the last they'll see of us. But we won't go until we finish what we've started."

"The preacher's watchin' us," Beeler said, a nervous sweat beginning to form on the back of his neck.

"Is he a pal of yours?"

"Somethin' like that. But he's had about all the disturbance he's goin' to stand for."

"We have no wish to disturb the funeral. All we want is to keep an eye on the Brannons until the services are over. Then, when the Indians go home, we'll take up the hunt again." Conmy smiled. "We'll even give them a few minutes' head start, to keep it sporting."

"I don't know anything about the Brannons," Beeler said grimly.

Conmy shrugged resignedly. “You leave us no choice; we’ll have to rout them out ourselves. If you interfere, Keating and Hump have their orders to start shooting. A thing like that would sort of play hell with the funeral, wouldn’t it?”

Beeler experienced the sensation of being slowly strangled. He didn’t trust himself to speak; and anyway, they had already attracted too much attention. He got to his feet, looked at them steadily in a way that would have caused more prudent men to shrink. Conmy and Sutter merely smiled. “Well,” Conmy said with a note of regret, “you can’t say we didn’t give you every chance.” Beeler walked blindly out of the church.

He was hardly out of the door when a strong hand took his arm. Light Horse Captain Forestman was looking down at him thoughtfully, coldly. “Who are the two men and the woman?”

Beeler wondered how much he could tell the Indian lawman without starting a war. “The woman is the wife of Mr. Conmy. You met Conmy and Sutter earlier out in the churchyard.”

That was no answer, and Forestman was well aware of it. “What do they want here?”

Beeler was on the point of telling him everything but at the last moment changed his mind. “I know them . . . slightly. Guided a hunting party for them once.”

Switching to Creek, Forestman told Beeler

about his friend John River, and his wife, who had been stopped and threatened by two white men. "Those two men were Conmy and Sutter. They were looking for outlaws—the Brannon bunch, Mr. River thinks." He paused for a moment and then asked, "Are those the Brannon brothers you've got in the camp house with you?"

Beeler sensed that this was not the time to lie. He nodded. "Yes."

The captain added the rest of it up for himself. Where there were outlaws with prices on their heads, there were sure to be bounty hunters. Bounty hunters were generally despised by everyone—as despised as the outlaws themselves, and sometimes more so. "I don't like it," he said bluntly, still speaking in Creek. "White bounty hunters, white outlaws." He shrugged his broad shoulders. "I understand why Preacher Hooker has agreed to help you. What I don't understand is why you have taken to palling with outlaws." He shrugged again. "But that's not important. Not to me. The thing that's important to me is my family. God help you, Marshal, if anything happens to give them more pain."

"I intend to see that the funeral is not disturbed."

"If it should be," the big Indian told him coldly, "you'll find no friend in the Creek Nation. I don't care what happens to your outlaw friends, or the bounty hunters, or you. I care only for my family and that they shouldn't be disturbed at this time of sadness." He added slowly, "I think you'd better get the Brannons out of the camp house."

"I can't do that. Conmy or Sutter would shoot them down before they got out of the churchyard."

Captain Forestman crossed his arms across his chest and became more distant, more Indian. "I leave it to you, then. After the funeral you and the outlaws and the bounty hunters can kill each other with my blessing. Until then, there will be no disturbance." With a curt nod he walked off toward the Forestman camp house.

Conmy and Sutter and Verna were coming out of the church now. They were smiling and blinking their eyes in the afternoon light. They looked for all the world, Beeler thought, like theatergoers who had just enjoyed a diverting new play and were not quite yet adjusted to the harsh reality of the world beyond the stage. They walked leisurely across the churchyard, chatting happily among themselves, quite oblivious—to the disapproving glances of the Indians. They came directly toward Beeler, as if he were an old friend and fellow theatergoer.

"I must say," Conmy said pleasantly, "that was the most interesting funeral I ever attended. Who is it that's dead, anyway? Couldn't be much more than a child, judging from the size of the casket."

"Who were the old men with the crooked staves?" Verna wanted to know. "They reminded me of pictures of the prophets that I used to look at in my mother's Bible." She looked brightly at Beeler. "I wonder if one of them would sell me his staff? Think of the sensation it would cause in Chicago."

"They would," Beeler told her stiffly, "rather sell their arms and legs."

"Will there be more services?" Ben Sutter wanted to know. "Or is it over now?"

"There'll be more, from time to time, as the family takes the notion." Beeler felt like a fool standing there in the churchyard talking like an old friend to people who had every intention of killing him.

"Good," Conmy said heartily. "We'll be sure to be here. I wouldn't want to miss anything."

"I wonder," Beeler said, "if it's ever occurred to you that the Indians might not want you here?"

All three of them showed surprise. How could anyone, least of all an Indian, bring himself to object to anything the Conmys or Sutters might take in their minds to do? As they pondered that minor mystery, Ben Sutter suddenly smiled and nudged Conmy. "Well, well! Warren, do you see what I see?"

Warren turned and let his gaze follow Ben's. A quick grin split his face. He sighed happily. "Mr. Leo Brannon, in person!" He turned and placed a friendly hand on Beeler's shoulder. "I don't mind telling you, this takes a load off my mind, Marshal." He chuckled quietly. "We'll be going now. If we should want you—or your friends—for anything, we know now where to find you."

With a sinking feeling in his gut, Beeler turned to look at the Waterman camp house which had suddenly captured so much attention. There on the doorstep sat Leo Brannon, gazing placidly at the clusters of mourners as they mingled in the churchyard.

In those dark moments just before dawn, the horn deacon sounded his four blasts, calling the mourners to this, the last day of the funeral. Verna, alone in her tent on the north bank of the Canadian, was awakened by the sound, and for perhaps the first time in her life she knew fear. It was a cold knot in her stomach and beaded sweat on her forehead. She sat bolt upright on the camp cot and heard her own voice calling shrilly, "Warren! Where are you?"

Warren was not there.

No one was there. The echo of the horn lingered in the timber, and when it was no longer audible to her ears, it lingered in her mind. It's only an old man, she told herself, blowing on a steerhorn. But the knot was still in her stomach. "What's wrong with me?" she demanded aloud, half in anger. "I've never been this way before."

She threw off the blanket and stood up, her bare feet prickling on the dry grass. She was appalled to note that she was trembling. In the past she had watched Warren kill wild animals at almost suicidal distances, and she had not trembled.

Somewhere in the darkness she heard someone running, making a great noise as he blundered through dense stands of weeds and brush. Someone threw back the flap of her tent and a tall figure stood in the opening. "Verna, are you all right?"

It was Duane Keating. Verna gasped, weak with relief, and almost fell into his arms. "Duane, I woke up and . . . Where's Warren?"

"Over at the clearing with Hump and Ben, keeping watch on the camp house where the Brannons are."

She shuddered and did not resist him as he put his arms around her. She was still trembling uncontrollably. In dismay she shook her head from side to side. "I don't know what's the matter with me. I was dreaming. And then that awful horn . . ."

"It was only the old man calling the Indians to church."

"I know, but there was something about it."

"It wasn't the horn, it must have been the dream. You'll be over it in a minute."

"The dream." She shuddered again. "I remember now. The casket. The one in the church. It was the funeral, and somebody opened the lid to the casket, and then everybody lined up to view the body. And when I got there, the body in the casket was Warren!"

"It was just a dream, Verna."

"Warren and Ben have got to stop this foolishness. You've got to make them stop it, Duane."

"I don't think I can. I don't think anyone can. You know how they are when they start a thing."

"You've got to try!" Her voice was rising toward hysteria.

"All right, Verna, I'll try. I'll go now and see what I can do."

"No!" The terror of the dream was still in her heart. "Wait a little while. I don't think I can stand being alone right now."

"All right," he said again, gently, as if he were soothing a frightened child. "I won't go until you're sure it's all right."

For a long while they stood there in the tent opening, unmoving, with the darkness of predawn surrounding them. From time to time Verna would shiver, remembering the dead face in the dream looking up at her from the small oak casket, and Keating would tighten his arms around her. How many times, he thought bleakly, I've wanted to hold you like this. But I was only your husband's secretary—it was unthinkable. Now it turns out it's not so unthinkable after all.

At last the darkness of the night began to recede, and with the darkness went most of Verna's fear. She blinked several times and made a startled little sound, as if amazed to find herself in Keating's arms. All at once it came to her how it must look, her bare feet prickling on the dry grass, the flimsy nightgown clinging to her body. Suddenly she pushed herself away. For once in her life Verna Conmy was unsure of herself; her face burned with embarrassment. "Duane," she said huskily, "you'd better go. Forget what I said—it was the dream. I was behaving like a fool."

He released her reluctantly. "Are you sure you're all right?"

"Of course, I'm sure." She was angry now. Angry at herself, at Keating, at the situation which was becoming more awkward and unexplainable by the second. In acute discomfort, she covered her face with her hands. "Go now, Duane! Just go!"

Now it was Keating's turn to glow with embarrassment at being snapped at, as if he were a servant. He stepped back quickly, awkward as a farmhand, knocking his hat off as he blundered through the tent opening. "All right, Verna," he said, recovering his hat, "whatever you say."

He wheeled and walked blindly into the timber. For some time he sat on a rotting stump and tried to pull himself together, sort out his thoughts and emotions. The feel of Verna was still with him. She had needed him—for a little while. When she thought she had lost Warren.

That's something to think about, he told himself quietly. And he sat there for a long while, with that one thought slowly growing in his mind.

CHAPTER TEN

The night passed in somber silence. Close friends and relatives of the Forestman family took turns sitting with the body inside the church; at nightfall most of the mourners began bedding down in camp houses and wagon beds and on the ground.

As night settled over the churchyard, Leo Brannon muttered for perhaps the hundredth time, "I'm beginnin' to think it was all a big mistake when me and Babe decided to leave the farm." He sat dejectedly in the gloom of the camp house, his elbows on the Waterman's cooktable. "Are you sure," he asked Beeler, "that them two dudes know where we're hidin'?"

"They know. They saw you sittin' on the doorstep."

"You think we ought to try to sneak away from here while it's dark?"

"They're watchin' this camp house like hawks. Show your face outside that door and they start shootin'."

The outlaw leader sighed miserably. In the middle of the churchyard someone had built a campfire to boil coffee for the men sitting with the body. Red light and black shadow danced on the camp houses. "If we could put out that fire," Babe Brannon said angrily, "might be we could get away without them seein' us."

"Forget it," Beeler told them. "They're not goin' to put out the fire, and we're not goin' to do anything to disturb the funeral."

Shortly after nightfall Brother Duel Hooker came to the camp house and called Beeler to the door. "Captain Forestman knows about the two outlaws you're protecting," he said in Creek.

"I know," Beeler said in the same language.

The preacher stood in the flickering light of the campfire, managing to look angry and sad at the same time. "I think you're being watched from the edge of the clearing," he said at last.

"I know. But they're not goin' to start a commotion as long as the funeral lasts. They don't have to; all they need to do is wait."

"What will you do tomorrow?"

"Attend the funeral, along with everybody else. If it's all right with the Forestmans."

The preacher looked down at the ground. "I don't understand any of this. You assure me that there will be no disturbance; yet there will be those men at the graveyard bent on killing you. How can there be no disturbance?"

Beeler smiled faintly. "I don't expect they'll shoot us down on the spot. Where would the sport be in that kind of killin'? No." He shook his head. "I figger they'll wait till the funeral's over and most everybody's gone from the graveyard. Then they'll give me and the Brannons a few minutes' start towards the timber. In a way we're lucky that

Conmy and Sutter are the kind of sportsmen they are—we might even get away from them, if we make it as far as the river."

Hooker stared at him without a trace of understanding. "Are you sure you aren't mistaken in your judgment of Conmy and Sutter? Hunting men down and killing them for sport—it's not sensible, it's not reasonable."

Beeler sighed to himself. "They're queer, dangerous men. There's nothin' sensible or reasonable about them."

The preacher suddenly looked very sad and old. Perhaps, Beeler thought, he was thinking about his son. "I owe you so much," he said softly, "and there's so little I can do."

"There's one thing you could do. Leave three saddle horses close to the entrance to the graveyard after the funeral's over."

Hooker nodded heavily. "I had already thought of that. Now you must do something for me—take no guns to the graveyard."

"Preacher," Beeler told him with feeling, "I want to go along with you as far as I can, but after that funeral's over, me and the Brannons are goin' to have to fight for our lives. We've got to have guns."

But Brother Hooker was shaking his head sternly. "No guns. I have given my word to Captain Forestman, and you must give me yours."

Beeler did some quick thinking. If nobody at all

brought guns to the graveyard, maybe that would be the best thing. With three good horses nearby, it was just possible that they might make a getaway without getting shot out of the saddle by Keating and O'Toole.

"Do I have your word?" the preacher pressed.

Grudgingly, Beeler nodded. In spite of all his reasoning, he would rather feel the weight of a good .45 next to his side. But the choice was not his; it belonged to Hooker and Captain Forestman.

"You *what?*" Leo Brannon hollered as soon as Beeler told them about the latest agreement with Hooker.

"No guns," Beeler told them wearily. "There's no sense arguin' about it. But think about it a minute; it might be the best thing that could happen. There'll be horses waitin' for us, as soon as the funeral's over. Even if Conmy and Sutter are there on the spot, there's not much they can do if the Indians disarm them."

"Ain't you forgettin' Keating and O'Toole?" Babe asked bitterly. "They'll have rifles."

Beeler sighed and shrugged his shoulders. "Boys, I never claimed that we wouldn't need a little luck."

The horn deacon sounded his four calls a few minutes before dawn. The last day of the funeral had begun.

Conmy and Sutter awoke from a brief sleep on the ground at the edge of the clearing. "Hump," Conmy said with a wide yawn, "how about stirring up some coffee? And you'd better see about Verna while you're at it. Ask her if she intends to attend the services this morning."

Ben Sutter was lounging beneath a cottonwood, idly watching the mourners file into the church. Conmy came and stood beside him, lighting an early morning cigar. "There's no doubt about Beeler and the Brannons still being in that camp shack, is there?"

"Hump and Keating have been keeping watch. Don't worry, they're still there."

"Then, by midafternoon it'll all be over."

"What if they decide to go with the Indians to the graveyard?"

"We'll go with them. Up till now we've been playing by the Indians' rules; they don't try to protect the outlaws, and we don't shoot up the funeral." He smiled. "We'll change the rules if we have to. But I don't think we will." He picked up his rifle and gazed fondly down its blue-steel barrel.

Ben Sutter gazed blandly out at the quiet scene in the churchyard. He was not particularly happy with the way this hunt was going. To his mind the benefits in sporting satisfaction did not justify the risks. The killing of a former deputy marshal was not likely to go unnoticed. Questions would be asked, investigations would be started. Any way you looked at it, it was a dangerous business.

Sutter was aware of Conmy watching him, quietly, thoughtfully, through a curtain of blue cigar smoke. "I see powerful thoughts in your head, Ben."

"I can't help wishing that Beeler had gone on to Arkansas when he had the chance."

Conmy sighed. "Well, he didn't." Suddenly he smiled and pointed with his cigar. Beeler had just stepped out of the camp house and was walking quickly across the churchyard. At the door of the *Mekko Sapkv Coko* he shook hands with several of the Indians. Then, with a quick look over his shoulder, he ducked into the church.

Conmy chuckled. "He's nervous."

"Maybe he's changed his mind about protecting the outlaws."

"Too late now," Conmy said with chill finality.

O'Toole returned with a blackened coffeepot and some granite cups. As the three of them stood at the edge of the clearing drinking the scalding coffee and thinking ahead to the afternoon and what would happen then, the strange, sweet sound of Creek singing came from the church. "Damn!" the butler said, wiping the back of his neck. "I wish they wouldn't make that kind of music."

But Conmy only smiled. It was music for the dead, and he found it appropriate to the occasion.

He asked, “Did you talk to Verna? Is she all right?”

“Mrs. Conmy said not to expect her for the services this morning; she’s had enough of Indian funerals for a while.”

Conmy laughed. “All right, but she’ll have to come this afternoon. I don’t want her staying in the tent by herself.”

At that moment Verna Conmy was standing just outside her tent. The morning sparkled with dew, and the haunting sound of the Creek singing drifted through the timber. She hugged herself in a woolen shawl while inching closer to the fire that Hump had built for her. The chill of the nightmare was still with her.

It was more than just the nightmare; there was the memory of Keating. What had he thought of her, throwing herself at him, in just her nightgown?

She was amazed to find that she was shivering. She despised herself for flying into a panic and acting the fool with her husband’s secretary. But that, she told herself, was over now. It had happened because of the dream—Keating himself had said so. But the thought lingered in the back of her mind: *Did Duane believe that?*

At that moment Duane Keating was still watching the rear of the camp house from the far edge of the clearing. The two outlaws inside the house did not interest him in the slightest—neither did Beeler, who had just entered the church. Whether they lived or died did not concern him at all, although he had good reason to believe that within a matter of hours, they would all be dead. That was the way Warren and Ben played the game. They did not play to lose.

Well, he thought with a still smile, there's a first time for everything.

From the camp house Leo and Babe Brannon listened dumbly as one of the visiting preachers took up a long, meandering prayer in a language they could not understand. After a while a woman from the Forestman camp house appeared with bowls of sofkee and wild-grape dumplings. Leo accepted the food without enthusiasm. "I'm beginnin' to get sick of possum grapes and Indian grits," the outlaw complained.

"Then don't eat it," Babe told him snappishly. "If them dudes get their way, we'll be dead before sundown. Don't hardly seem worth goin' to the trouble of eatin'!"

Nevertheless, they did eat, cleaning the bowls thoroughly, leaving nothing for Beeler. "What we ought to do," Leo said, picking grape seeds out of his teeth with the point of his barlow knife, "is light out of here as fast as we can. Head for the timber and make ourselves so scarce that there wouldn't *nobody* ever find us."

Babe snorted. "We wouldn't get four steps from this shack. Them dudes and their fancy rifles."

Both men folded their arms across their chests and glared resolutely into space. That was the way Beeler found them when he returned from the prayer service. "Well," Leo demanded the instant Beeler stepped through the doorway, "have you figgered a way to get us out of this mess you got us into?"

Beeler stared at him. "*I* got you into?"

"You brought them murderin' dudes into the Territory, didn't you? Whose fault is it, if it ain't yours?"

Beeler decided immediately that there would be no profit in pursuing that line of thought. "No matter who got you into it," he said patiently, "you're in it now. And so am I. But there's still a chance we'll come out with our hides on. With a little luck, and some help from the preacher."

Immediately after the noontime meal, the horn deacon called the congregation for the last act of the service for the dead. Brother Duel Hooker appeared at the doorway of the camp house. He looked at Beeler and the outlaws with dark, sad eyes. "There will be a brief service in the church," he said in Creek to Beeler. "Then the congregation will view the body before taking it to the burial ground. You understand that this will be a very difficult time for the Forestmans; no disturbance of any kind will be tolerated."

Beeler nodded. "I understand."

"Do your friends intend to go to the burial ground with the rest of us?"

"If it's all right with the Forestmans."

The preacher nodded gravely. It was then that they saw Ben Sutter and the Conmys stroll out of the timber and start across the churchyard. Brother Hooker regarded them bleakly. "I wish," he told Beeler in his own language, "that there was some way I could help you. But my entire concern now is for the Forestmans."

"I understand," Beeler said, looking at Verna Conmy moving regally on the arms of her husband and brother. I hope *they* understand, he thought to himself. But he had little hope that they would.

The preacher looked back at Beeler. For several seconds he appeared to turn something over in his mind. "Sometime yesterday," he said at last, "Captain George Forestman left his family at the camp house, and they haven't seen him since. Did he speak to you before he left?"

Beeler shook his head. "No. Why should he?"

"No reason. Well . . ." He nodded again. "I'll be going now." Beeler took it as a rare compliment that the preacher had not again mentioned guns. He had given his word, and that was enough. The Indians still regarded him as a man of some honor, and that was something.

"I wish that preacher would talk American like everybody else," Leo complained as Hooker walked away. "What did he want this time?"

"I'm not sure," Beeler said slowly. "I think he came to tell us that the Light Horse captain disappeared sometime yesterday and hasn't been seen since. It's not like George to go off from his family at a time like this—it's got to be somethin' important."

He had caught the two outlaws' attention. "Important how?" Babe demanded. When Beeler only shrugged, he asked hopefully, "Would he be roundin' up some more Indian police to ride herd on this funeral?"

"Maybe." But Beeler didn't really think so. Indian police made it a rule to attend strictly to Indian affairs; whites were the business of the federal courts. "I don't think," he said dryly, "that we'd better count on the Indians to get us out of this."

"Who *do* we count on?"

"Ourselves." He was watching Sutter and the Conmys standing all by themselves in front of the church. The Indians simply pretended that they were invisible. This was not the first time that white men had intruded into their personal lives; there was little under the law that could be done about it, so they had long since decided the best way to deal with them was to ignore them.

This didn't seem to bother Conmy or Sutter, but

Verna seemed ill at ease with so many dark, cold eyes looking straight through her. Beeler smiled faintly to himself; he knew what it was like to be an invisible white man in a crowd of Indians. He had been one himself once, before Tom Hooker's trouble.

"How do you figger we're goin' to help ourselves?" Babe Brannon asked with growing impatience.

Beeler realized that his thoughts had been wandering. "We'll do nothin' until after the burial. Neither will Conmy or Sutter, if they've got half the sense I think they've got. After the casket is in the grave, the crowd will start breakin' up. If we're going to save our hides, it has to be then. Off to the west of the graveyard there's the north fork of the Canadian. Plenty of timber, plenty of places to lay low for maybe two, three hours, till night comes."

He looked to see how they were taking it. Leo shrugged dejectedly. "If that preacher has saddle animals waitin' for us, might be it would work." But he didn't sound hopeful.

"Ain't you forgettin' them other two dudes again?" Babe asked. "The sharpshooters with the rifles?"

"I'm not forgettin' them, but Keating and O'Toole are not part of the game. Conmy and Sutter are the hunters, Keating and O'Toole merely the beaters. Of course," Beeler shrugged, "if the game starts to go sour, Keating and O'Toole might start doin' some killin' of their own. But I'm bettin' that Conmy and Sutter will want to keep it a sportin' proposition, if they can. Even if it means losin' us in the timber for a while."

Across the churchyard two deacons and four husky young Creeks came out of the church and approached Sutter and the Conmys. Scowling, Conmy listened to what the Indians had to say. Then he looked at Sutter, and the two young men shrugged together. Apparently the Creeks were giving them the choice of leaving the churchyard or turning over their weapons. They hesitated for a moment, glancing back toward the river where Keating and O'Toole would be watching the little scene over the sights of their rifles. With a little grin of resignation, Conmy reached for his shoulder holster and handed over his little double-action revolver. A moment later Sutter did the same.

Leo Brannon, observing the scene from the doorway of the camp house, grunted his approval. "Boys," he said to the world at large, "it might just be that the Brannons will come out of this with their hides on after all."

"Put your guns on the table," Beeler told them.

Reluctantly, the two outlaws hauled their revolvers out of their waistbands and put them on the Waterman cooktable. "It's time we got started," Beeler said with a brisk self-assurance that he didn't feel.

As Beeler and Babe stepped out of the camp house, Leo hesitated in the doorway. For a moment he wrestled with himself; but only for a moment. "I ain't goin' to mix with them murderin' dudes," he thought angrily, "without a gun!" Quickly, he grabbed up his .45 and hid it under his shirt.

Conmy and Sutter appeared to have recovered from the brief shock of having their pistols taken from them. The two men stood in the center of the churchyard watching Beeler and the outlaws coming toward them. They had wide smiles on their faces. Warren Conmy nodded pleasantly to Beeler while Sutter and Verna stared with open curiosity at the two outlaws.

"I must say"—Conmy smiled—"you've led us an interesting chase, Marshal. A funeral!" He laughed. "Who could imagine a more fitting way to end a hunt."

"Hunt!" Babe Brannon muttered angrily. "Is that what you called it when you dry-gulched Rafe Jackson and John Coyotesong? Murder's what I call it."

Conmy seemed genuinely shocked by Babe's outburst. "Murder?" He sounded as if the word had an unpleasant taste in his mouth. "If I wished it, my servants would kill you at this very moment, just where you stand. *That* would be murder. As it is, Mr. Sutter and myself have decided to give you a five-minute start toward the woods, as soon as the funeral is over, before we take up our rifles. That is sport, Mr. Brannon, not murder."

Leo Brannon's face darkened. "I'll tell you somethin', mister, I'm gettin' goddamn sick of this *sport* of yours!"

Alarmed, Beeler grabbed the outlaw's arm in an ironlike grip and quickly steered him toward the church. "Save some of that bile for later!" he hissed. "You'll need it!"

Inside the church the deacon-usher directed Beeler and the angry Brannons, then Conmy and Sutter, to the bench reserved for male visitors. Across the aisle Verna sat alone and pale. It seemed to Beeler that Verna was not as amused as she had been the previous day.

But Conmy and Sutter, their interest and curiosity rekindled, gazed about in wide-eyed delight. An old man shuffled down the aisle, a picture of ancient dignity, his vest buttoned up wrong and his hat still on his head. Conmy nudged his brother-in-law and both young men laughed silently. It seemed that they had completely forgotten Leo's angry outburst in the churchyard.

Slowly, the church filled to capacity. Those who could not get in gathered outside near the door, and those inside began fanning themselves with palmetto leaves. The air was stifling; Beeler began to wish that the old parson would get the service started.

But the old man sat like a frail rag doll in his big chair behind the pulpit. The preacher, the visiting preachers, the licensed minister, the deacons, and the class leaders, all had taken their places and were waiting. The Forestman family, in a section of its own, was in its place, with the single exception of Captain George Forestman. It seemed that every place was occupied; some Creek matrons had even seated themselves on the bench normally reserved for female visitors. Verna Conmy, surrounded by Indians, had lost a good deal of her queenly self-assurance. She looked nervous and vaguely frightened, and Beeler wondered why. What could frighten a Sutter or a Conmy?

And still the old parson sat, apparently asleep in his carved oak chair. Brother Hooker and the other preachers sat beside him in their lesser chairs, ramrod straight and staring straight ahead. There was a moment of quiet sobbing in the Forestman section, otherwise the only sound in the small building was the rustle of palmetto fans stirring the sluggish air. The blanket of summer flowers on the casket filled the room with sad perfume.

Conmy nudged Beeler with his elbow and asked, "What's the old man waiting on?"

Beeler refused to look at him or answer him. Ben Sutter leaned forward and grinned. "I think he's gone to sleep. Or maybe he's dead."

They sat back on the bench and silently chuckled at their little joke while fanning themselves with their hats. Leo Brannon, on Beeler's other side, angrily mopped his sweaty face and hissed into Beeler's ear, "What's the hold up here?"

"The old parson's not ready yet. I guess he's got his reasons."

"I got as much respect for the dead as the next man," the outlaw complained under his breath, "but I'd just as soon get this funeral over with."

"The longer they take," Beeler reminded him, "the closer it'll be to night when we get to the graveyard, and the better our chances will be."

There was a stir of activity in the churchyard. The crowd at the doorway parted and the towering figure of George Forestman entered the church and strode down the aisle to the section reserved for his family. He was dusty and sweaty and had obviously just come in from a hard ride. His spurs made a jarring, unseemly racket in that quiet room.

Leo gave Beeler a nervous nudge with his elbow. "What's that Light Horse lawman up to?"

Beeler motioned for him to be quiet. Captain Forestman, after hesitating briefly in front of the small casket, took his place in the family section. Only then did the little parson push himself to his feet and approach the pulpit. In the language of the Creeks he addressed the Forestmans and only the

Forestmans; the other mourners might not have been there at all for all the attention he gave them.

He spoke softly and serenely of *Hesaketumese* who was now welcoming the soul of the dead boy into Heaven. He read reassuring passages from the Creek Bible and offered a short prayer. Beeler could see that it was going to be a brief service. The parson nodded to the head deacon, the head deacon stepped forward and raised the lid of the coffin.

Leo turned to Beeler in surprise. "Is it over?"

Beeler nodded.

The congregation, with the exception of the Forestman family, stood, and one of the class leaders began the first chilling notes of "Illka Este?" The rest of the congregation took up the singing, and the mourners outside the church began filing down the aisle. At the open casket each mourner paused for a moment to say his silent good-by to young Jack Forestman.

After the overflow of mourners had passed by the casket, a deacon motioned with his staff for Beeler to start a second procession. Beeler moved into the aisle, followed by the two nervous outlaws and Conmy and Sutter. They filed past the casket, glancing briefly at the blank, dead face of a boy they had never known, and then moved back up the other aisle to the door and finally to the churchyard.

Conmy and Sutter, again forming their quiet

little island in a sea of Indians, were perfectly relaxed and chatting animatedly about the service. Leo Brannon grasped Beeler's arm and muttered from the side of his mouth, "I say we ought to make a run for it right now!"

"Not," Beeler told him grimly, "unless you just *want* to get yourselves shot. If Keating and O'Toole didn't kill you, the Forestmans would."

The outlaw pulled out a filthy bandana and mopped his sweaty face. "I don't like the way that Light Horseman didn't show up till the last minute. What's he been up to?"

Conmy and Sutter had broken off their cheerful discussion of the funeral service. They sauntered casually over to Beeler and the outlaws. "An interesting day," Sutter said pleasantly.

"But it's almost over," Conmy observed, looking closely at Beeler and the Brannons. Looking for signs of fear, Beeler thought. Conmy smiled and seemed pleased with the glitter of anxiety and danger in the eyes of the Brannon brothers. It added a certain spice to what might otherwise be a routine kill.

The Creeks were beginning to bring up their saddle horses and wagons in preparation for the final procession to the graveyard. Brother Duel Hooker, seeing the grim look on Beeler's face, appeared suddenly beside him. "I have your word, Marshal. You're to do nothing to disturb these services."

Beeler sighed. “You have my word.”

“You must trust more in the Lord,” the preacher said dryly.

“It looks like He’s all I’ve got left.”

“You have my friendship, and the friendship of many others here today. As for your other friends . . .” He gazed coolly at the Brannons and shrugged. “Anyhow, have a little faith, Marshal.”

“Look here, if you and George Forestman have been up to somethin’, I want to know about it.”

“Just remember what I tell you,” the tall preacher said. “Trust in the Lord. In the meantime, I hold you to your word.”

“Even if it gets me shot?”

“No matter what,” Hooker told him.

CHAPTER ELEVEN

At the edge of the clearing Duane Keating and Humphrey O'Toole watched over the sights of their rifles as the mourners filed slowly out of the church. O'Toole grunted as he centered the front bead on Frank Beeler's broad chest. It was his job to kill Beeler instantly if the former marshal should try to get the drop on Conmy or Sutter. It was a job that he was prepared to do quickly and efficiently but with no particular relish.

O'Toole shot a quick glance at Keating who, at the moment, had his rifle resting in the fork of a wild-plum sapling. "Keep your eyes open," the butler snapped. "Looks like the funeral's breaking up."

Keating did not answer, but the quick spots of color in his cheeks suggested that he did not enjoy taking orders from a servant. At that moment he had his rifle aimed steadily at the back of Leo Brannon's head, but his thoughts were not on the outlaw. From the corner of his eye he watched Verna Conmy coming out of the church. Her face looked pale and drawn; she seemed to be floating on a dark river of Indians. Why had Warren brought her here today? Keating angrily asked himself. She hadn't wanted to come. The effects of the nightmare were still upon her, and she had asked to be left behind at camp. But to this Warren would not agree. Today, if everything went according to plan, would be the highlight of his career as a hunter; he wanted his wife with him.

Almost as if it had a will of its own, the muzzle of Keating's rifle moved away from Leo Brannon. It swept slowly past the long, unhappy face of Babe Brannon, hesitated for just an instant on the bland, smiling countenance of Ben Sutter. At last the bead sight came to a stop, resting on the left pocket of Warren Conmy's Bedford-cord jacket.

"Keating!"

The secretary jumped, almost dropped his rifle. The red-faced O'Toole was glaring at him angrily. "What do you think you're doing? I told you to keep an eye on those two outlaws!"

Keating could feel the blood draining from his face. He found that his hands were sweaty. There were great wet blotches on the rifle where he had been holding it in a death's grip.

O'Toole was scowling at him darkly. "Since the Indians took Mr. Conmy's and Mr. Sutter's pistols," he said angrily, "they'll be relying on us more than ever. If you can't follow your employer's orders, I suggest you resign from his service."

The secretary looked at him. "I can follow orders."

"Then do it," O'Toole snapped. "Don't stand there gaping, with your attention wandering all over the churchyard."

For a moment Keating looked at the butler so steadily and coldly that O'Toole took an involuntary step back from his supporting tree trunk. What he glimpsed in those still blue eyes he could not give name to, but it brought a dry prickle to his skin and a twist in his gut. Once a beautiful and deadly little coral snake had crawled over O'Toole's bare foot, and he had experienced the same fleeting unpleasantness. Unconsciously, he reached for a handkerchief and moved it around on his red face. "Well," he added lamely, after the angry outburst, "keep your mind on the business at hand today."

The glossy leaves of the cottonwoods rustled noisily in a slight breeze. O'Toole did not look in Keating's direction but paid strict attention to the activity in the churchyard. Indians were still filing out of the church; they walked haughtily past Sutter and the Conmys, without even looking in their direction. It was clear that they resented the presence of the white men whose only purpose in being here, as it seemed, was to be entertained. But they made nothing of their resentment, busying themselves with saddling horses and hitching teams.

O'Toole noted that some of the Indians nodded to Beeler in a civil, almost friendly way, but ignored the two outlaws at his side. As far as the butler could tell, none of the Indians was armed. That, anyway, was something to be thankful for.

"Here it comes," the butler said quietly to no one in particular. Six Creek men, led by the head deacon and class leader, bore the casket out of the church and placed it in the bed of a waiting wagon.

Once again O'Toole was all business. Any trace of apprehension that he might have experienced earlier was now well behind him. "Bring up the horses," he snapped to the secretary, "it's time we got started."

With no show of resentment, Keating quickly jogged back into the timber and brought up the saddle animals. O'Toole was grinning, nodding toward the clearing. "Look at that. The hunter and the hunted riding to a funeral in the same wagon. Leave it to Mr. Conmy and Mr. Sutter to put the odd twist to a hunt."

"I don't think Mr. Conmy or Mr. Sutter had much to do with it," the secretary said dryly.

And Keating was right. Captain George Forestman, with the grim air of a man who would tolerate no nonsense, ordered the Conmys, Sutter, the two Brannons, and Beeler all into the same wagon. To make sure there would be no disturbance, he got in with them.

Conmy and Sutter didn't seem to mind being thrown together with the men they intended to kill. They stood behind the Indian driver, with Verna between them, gazing with keen interest at everything that happened. Ben Sutter glanced toward the timber and said with a note of mild relief, "Well, it's almost over. How long do you think it'll take to get to the graveyard?"

Conmy shrugged. "Not long. Plenty of time to get the burial over with and get the Indians started back toward their homes. Before dark the game will be over."

"You make it sound so matter of fact," Sutter said dryly. "I hope you realize that this is not quite the same as shooting ducks from a blind. At the moment we're unarmed and helpless—and we'll remain that way until we somehow manage to get our rifles from Keating and O'Toole."

"So the chase will last a little longer than we'd planned." Conmy laughed softly. "Are you getting nervous, Ben?"

Sutter shrugged. "No. Just so we realize that, in this kind of hunt, the hunter too could get killed."

The wagon bearing the casket pulled away from the church and made its way toward a narrow wagon track in the timber. A wagon bearing the Forestman family wheeled in behind, followed by horsebackers and more wagons. "Yes, sir," Warren Conmy said, beaming expectantly, "it'll soon be over."

In the back of the wagon the Brannon brothers were getting more nervous by the minute. "I tell you," Leo said angrily, "them two dudes has got some kind of scheme up their sleeves. The Indians took their pistols away from them, didn't they? What have they got to be grinnin' about?"

Beeler said patiently, "Don't let them get you rattled. There's nothin' they can do until they get their hands on some rifles. We'll have a good start on them by that time."

"And their murderin' little game'll be right back where it started."

"But we'll still be alive." *I hope,* Beeler added silently.

George Forestman was watching them casually but without any real interest. Beeler looked at him quietly, waiting for something—but he didn't know what. They had been friends for a long while, Beeler and the Forestman family, but he knew very well that any friendship between a Creek and a white man was a fragile thing at best. He doubted that the captain cared much how many white men were killed today, so long as they waited until after the funeral to do it.

Well, Beeler thought to himself, I can't say that I can blame him much for that.

Babe Brannon nudged Beeler and pointed down a grassy slope to the timbered banks of the river. Two horsebackers were slipping in and out between the trees. One of them rode with a curiously stiff leg, the stirrup held out at an improbable angle as the man hunched forward in the saddle. Humphrey O'Toole. The second rider was deeper in the timber and was visible only as a dark shadow, but Beeler had no doubt that it was Keating.

Conmy and Sutter had also seen the horsemen. They looked toward the rear of the wagon and smiled.

The Creek graveyard was a small, neat plot on the side of a small hill, no more than a hundred yards from the north fork of the Canadian. It was a strange, eerie experience seeing one of the Indian graveyards for the first time. Each grave was covered by a small house, the home for the spirit of the dead person. The cemetery looked like a small, silent city, with wildflowers growing in the streets. Here the only sound was the whisper of wind in the grass; it could be unnerving.

Some of the gravehouses were new and freshly painted, some were old and in ruins. A derelict gravehouse could not be repaired; it was believed that the older the house the newer the spirit—a theological subtlety that not many white men fully understood. Each gravehouse had a small window at the head, which always faced west. The body to go into the grave was bare of foot and clad in cotton; it was not known exactly why, except that wool was of the lamb and as such was forbidden.

The procession stopped at the edge of the graveyard, the casket was taken to the new grave where the deacons, class leaders, parson, and preachers prepared for the last sad farewell to young Jack Forestman. The mourners got down from horses and wagons and filed silently to the open grave. Beeler couldn't help looking back over his shoulder at the heavy stand of oak and walnut and cottonwood bordering the river. Down there somewhere Keating and O'Toole were waiting.

The big Light Horse captain dropped down to the ground and, with Warren Conmy, handed Verna down from the wagon. "This last service is mostly a family affair," he told the white visitors in his strangely stilted English. "You are welcome, of course, but please stand over there." He indicated the place with a nod. "There on the slope behind the Forestman family and its old friends."

Beeler looked at the captain—he knew of no rule about who should stand where at a grave ceremony. The captain looked back at him with dark blankness.

The mourners filed silently into the graveyard and stood beside the open grave. George carefully herded the white visitors to their place, and Beeler saw with some relief that they now had the entire congregation between themselves and the river. Until the ceremony broke up and the Indians left the hillside, there was very little that O'Toole and Keating could do, rifles or no rifles.

When Forestman was satisfied that everybody was in place, he came to Beeler and smiled with a kind of wry sadness. "No need," he said quietly in Creek, "to worry about the riflemen on the riverbank."

Beeler tried not to look surprised, but it was a moment before he could think of anything to say. "Well," he managed at last, "if you know about Keating and O'Toole, you must know they're something to worry about."

"Not today. A United States marshal and three possemen will see to that."

Beeler stiffened with anger. "So *that's* where you went yesterday. To bring back a deputy marshal. I had Preacher Hooker's word that he wouldn't do anything like that."

"You didn't have my word." At graveside the old parson was thumbing through his Bible, about to begin this last brief service. "I know that my family is indebted to you, Marshal," the captain went on quickly, "but I could not allow a killing here, at this time, at this place. If you're involved with the outlaws, I'm sorry."

"I'm not involved," Beeler said, louder than he intended. "Not the way you think. But I promised to help them."

The big lawman nodded. "I think I understand. I know about bounty hunters." He still thought that Conmy and Sutter were bounty hunters. "Well, the bounty hunters won't harm anyone; the marshal and his men will close in as soon as the service is over. The Brannons will be arrested by a United States marshal and tried in a federal court. Surely you can't object to that?"

There was a great deal that Beeler could have objected to. For one thing he was guilty of harboring wanted outlaws which, in the eyes of the courts, made him an outlaw himself and liable to arrest. The big Light Horseman shrugged and said regretfully, "I know you think this is poor payment for the service you've done for young Tom Hooker and for my own family. But a Creek funeral is a sacred matter, not a circus for the entertainment of white bounty hunters, nor a refuge for white outlaws." He sighed and spread his hands. "Do you understand?"

Beeler set his jaw and said nothing.

"Well," the captain went on wearily, "I did what seemed best for my family. I notified Marshal Gifford. He's down in the timber somewhere, and the riflemen of Conmy and Sutter are under arrest. Three of Gifford's possemen have mixed with the congregation; as soon as the funeral is over they'll move in quietly and put the outlaws under arrest." At that moment the old parson began to read a passage from his Creek Bible, and the captain moved away.

At Beeler's side Babe Brannon had listened in frustration and anger to the exchange between the Light Horseman and Beeler. "What was *that* about?" he hissed from the side of his mouth. "What're you and that Indian policeman schemin' together now?"

Beeler shot him a look of anger and motioned him to shut up.

Reluctantly, the outlaw shut his mouth, but he fidgeted nervously and shot anxious glances in the direction of the river.

Beside the open grave the old parson closed his Bible and spoke a few quiet words to the Forestman family. Then Brother Duel Hooker looked up for a moment at the dazzling sky and started what promised to be a long and powerful prayer.

Beeler neither listened to the words nor looked at the preacher. He thought about what George Forestman had told him. With Keating and O'Toole and their deadly rifles out of the game, he should have experienced a powerful sensation of relief. Even if they arrested him, he had little doubt that he could somehow square himself in Fort Smith. Conmy and Sutter's murderous little "game" was over. Beeler should have been offering a prayer himself, of thankfulness.

But the truth was that he didn't feel relieved at all. Little ripples of anxiety raced up his back. Oily beads of nervous sweat formed on his forehead. He looked around for some sign of the marshal's possemen. He couldn't spot them, but there was no reason to believe that they weren't somewhere in the crowd. As soon as the service was over, he could think of no reason why the lawmen couldn't move in quickly and quietly and arrest the Brannons. That would be the end of it. The Brannons would go to prison; the two sportsmen, their "game" still unfinished, could go wherever they pleased.

Still there was something about it that Beeler didn't trust. He turned and looked for several seconds toward the river. There was no movement in the timber that he could detect. Well, he told himself, that was the way it was supposed to be. If the lawmen had taken O'Toole and Keating into custody, the riverbank had every right to be still and undisturbed.

Preacher Hooker's final prayer for young Jack Forestman sounded as if it might go on for the rest of the afternoon. Beeler turned his gaze to George Forestman, who was now standing beside the grave with his family. The straight back and broad shoulders told Beeler nothing.

Before the funeral party arrived at the graveyard, Keating and O'Toole had already stationed themselves near the edge of the timber. O'Toole had selected the place for its uninterrupted view of the cemetery. Everything was within easy rifle range—if Conmy and Sutter got themselves into trouble, the butler and the secretary were in position to offer covering fire with deadly effect.

Up on the grassy slope three gravediggers, friends of the Forestman family, were just finishing the new grave. They squared the corners and smoothed the sides with meticulous care, as though they were creating a lasting work of art. O'Toole took a practice sighting on the broad brown face of the nearest workman and grunted with satisfaction. He was a man without imagination or humor; he served his master as uncomplainingly as a machine. And he never questioned the rightness of anything that Warren Conmy might propose.

"There," O'Toole said suddenly, his head cocked alertly. "Did you hear something?"

Keating shook his head. "No."

"I heard something," the butler said, scowling. He shoved himself to his feet and stumped to the edge of the clearing.

"It can't be the burial party," Keating said without interest. "They haven't had time to get this far."

"All the same, I heard something," O'Toole insisted. Quietly, he jacked a cartridge into the breach of his rifle.

"An animal," Keating suggested, still not very interested.

O'Toole shook his head. "Go back to the river and see if anyone's coming."

It rankled Keating to take orders from a servant; still, if someone had followed them to the graveyard, he wanted to know about it. He moved quietly through the undergrowth to the edge of the water.

There was nothing there. No animal, no wandering Indian, nothing. *And yet . . .*

Suddenly the air was dry and electric. The secretary wheeled and tried to get O'Toole's attention, but the butler had frozen in an attitude of concentration; he was aware of nothing but the sound that had first disturbed him. It was then that Keating first saw Marshal Sid Gifford crawling on all fours through a stand of dark green mullein.

Keating reacted instinctively. The stock of his rifle seemed to jump to his shoulder; within a matter of seconds he had the lawman in his sights. He recognized Gifford at once as the marshal who had once trapped the Brannon outlaws and then let them get away. Evidently, the lawman was in no mood to let them get away again. On his face there was a mask of long-standing anger. For a moment he paused in his crawling march through the mullein and regarded O'Toole with such cold hatred that Keating flinched.

The secretary's finger was firm on the trigger, but a voice in some far corner of his mind warned him not to start shooting unnecessarily. For one thing, shooting a United States marshal was not a thing to be taken lightly. Also, it was clear that the lawman was not aware of Keating's presence.

Well, Keating thought with a grim little smile,

maybe it would be wise to wait and see what the lawman had in mind.

He lowered his rifle and moved quietly back into the brush, but not so far back that he could not see both O'Toole and the marshal. Gifford paused and rested for a moment on one elbow. Then he lifted his hand a few inches in what was clearly a signal of some sort. Keating scowled, puzzled. But in a moment the mystery cleared—about twenty yards upstream a second figure was taking shape in the leafy undergrowth behind O'Toole.

Now Keating was beginning to understand what was happening. The marshal had somehow learned that the Brannons were going to be at the graveyard at this particular time. Gifford was clearly a man intent on collecting that bounty, and he did not intend for O'Toole or anybody else to interfere with that objective.

The secretary allowed himself a moment to size up the situation. If the lawman managed to capture or kill O'Toole without alerting the funeral party, it logically followed that the Brannon brothers would fall to the marshal, not to Warren and Ben.

Keating found this prospect highly satisfying. He could well imagine the rage that would possess the huntsmen when they realized that their diversion had been spoiled at the last moment.

Keating watched with lively interest as Marshal Sid Gifford lay almost flat in the weeds. "Drop the rifle, mister," the lawman called in a brisk, businesslike voice. "I'm a deputy United States marshal."

O'Toole wheeled on his peg leg and almost fell. He stared at the dense mullein in alarm; his beet-red face had paled to a flaming pink.

The posseman who had been moving up to O'Toole's rear, stood up suddenly and leveled his own rifle at the butler. "Do like he says! Unless you want to get dropped in a cross fire!"

Keating could see the sweat glistening on O'Toole's face. The butler gripped his rifle determinedly, waiting for the secretary to step in and spring the marshal's trap.

But Keating did not move.

"Your last chance, mister," Gifford said in a voice that was both calm and deadly.

O'Toole hesitated for perhaps five seconds, and then he realized that Keating was not going to come to his aid. Perhaps Keating had also been trapped; he had no way of knowing.

The only thing that O'Toole was absolutely sure of was that he was in an excellent way to die in a cross fire. As he was no fool, the butler dropped his rifle.

Gifford rose up in the weed patch, his rifle leveled at O'Toole's chest. "Make sure he ain't got a pistol."

The posseman—a big, rawboned farm hand—moved up cautiously on O'Toole's right. He grinned at the butler, flashing a row of yellow teeth. Keating—even from a distance of almost forty yards—imagined that he could see the glint of greed in the posseman's eyes. No doubt he too had heard about the Brannon bounty.

"Now then," Gifford was saying comfortably, the muzzle of his rifle drooping just a little. "See about the pistol, Roy."

Roy moved to O'Toole's left. He was still grinning and holding his rifle in both hands as if it were a club. Without a breath of warning, he lifted the weapon and smashed the heavy stock against the butler's head.

Keating was shocked. Killing a man from a distance, clean and quick, with a beautiful rifle, was one thing—poleaxing him, as if he were a steer in a slaughter pen, was something quite different. In an angry flash he had the sights of his own rifle centered on the posseman's grinning face—but the warning voice in the back of his mind spoke sharply. *Don't act hastily! After all, what is O'Toole to you?*

The answer to that was simple. *Nothing.*

He watched coolly now, without emotion, as the butler's face went suddenly blank. O'Toole fell gracelessly, his peg leg flying out at an awkward angle. After his crashing fall, the butler did not move again.

Marshal Sid Gifford reacted with mild irritation. "What the hell did you go and do that for?"

"We couldn't have him makin' a fuss, could

we?" the posseman asked innocently. "If there's a fuss and shootin', then the funeral gets busted up. And the Brannons run off before we ever get a crack at them. Or them two dude bounty hunters will kill them. Then where would *we* be?"

"Without a bounty," Keating thought with a tight little grin.

Evidently the marshal was thinking the same thing. He waded through the weeds and stood for a moment over O'Toole's still form. "Well," he said with a shrug, "I guess there's no sense frettin' about it now. Where did Brian and Milo get to?"

"Scoutin' the river, lookin' for the other dude."

The lawman tucked his rifle under his arm, dug in his pocket for makings and began building a smoke. For several minutes the two men stood there near the edge of the timber, idly watching the gravediggers. At last there was some movement downstream and two possemen came crashing carelessly through the undergrowth. They were two hungry-looking farm boys, like the first one.

"Me and Milo scoured the whole bottom," one of them said wearily. "There ain't anybody within shootin' distance of this graveyard. You sure that Light Horseman said there was two?"

Gifford shrugged. "That's what he said, but you can't believe everything an Indian tells you. Well," he added, nudging the unconscious butler with the toe of his boot, "we won't have to worry about this one for a spell. Did you see anything of the funeral party?"

"They're comin', maybe two hundred all told. In wagons and on horseback mostly, but a few on foot."

"Did you see the Brannons?"

The man called Milo laughed. "We seen them. And the woman, too—Conmy's woman, I guess, that the Light Horseman told us about. All loaded in the same wagon with Beeler and Conmy and Sutter. And the Indian policeman. What's his name?"

"Forestman."

"That's the one. Well, he's holdin' up his end of the bargain, anyhow. He's deliverin' the Brannons to the graveyard, like he said he would. Do you think we're goin' to have to fight them bounty hunters, Conmy and Sutter?"

Gifford grinned. "We ain't goin' to fight nobody at all. The two dudes got their pistols took away from them. And this one . . ." He gave O'Toole another kick. "He ain't goin' to be much help to anybody for quite a spell."

The posseman shrugged. "Just so we get the two Brannons. And the bounty. I don't guess it makes much difference when we do it."

The four men formed a little half circle around the still form of Humphrey O'Toole and watched with idle curiosity as the gravediggers cleaned their shovels. Marshal Gifford was not particularly worried about the outcome of the affair. The Light Horseman had set it up for them, and it looked like Forestman was sticking to his word. No fuss or commotion at the funeral. That had been the marshal's promise to the Indian. And the Brannons were theirs. That was the bargain.

Everything was simple and straightforward; it was hard to see how anything could go wrong.

There were the dude bounty hunters to think about, of course, but Gifford didn't anticipate any trouble there. He had crossed trails with eastern dudes before and nothing in his experience gave him any reason to worry about Conmy and Sutter.

"Here they come," the posseman called Roy said to no one in particular. In the distance they could hear the creak of ungreased wagon wheels. The four men looked at one another and grinned. They were—in their own minds—already spending the bounty money.

Beside the newly dug grave the three workmen had finished cleaning their shovels and were now kneeling in prayer.

The wagon bearing the small oak casket lumbered out of the timber and lurched along the rutted wagon track toward the graveyard. Marshal Gifford, dismissing the possibility that O'Toole had had a partner, spoke briskly. "All right, it's time we got down to business. I can't go up there and mix with the Indians; too many Indians know me. I'll lay back here out of sight and keep my rifle on the Brannons. Roy, when the crowd starts to gather, you and Brian and Milo mix in with the others and keep an eye on the outlaws. As soon as the service is over, throw down on them. If they make a fuss, kill them. Brian, you keep a watch on Beeler and the two dudes. I don't figger they'll make any trouble, but if they do—kill them. I don't aim for the Brannon brothers to get away from me this time."

Roy scratched his bristling jaw. "What about the Indians?"

"Don't start a ruckus before the service is over, and there won't be any trouble. An Indian has got more sense than to mix in with white men's troubles."

"That Creek policeman said he didn't want any guns at the graveyard."

"You don't have to do everything an Indian tells you, do you? Take your pistols, but keep them out of sight."

As the wagons gathered alongside the graveyard, the three possemen stacked their rifles, tucked their pistols in their waistbands under their shirts, and quietly mixed with the milling crowd.

Marshal Gifford took a practice sighting on the Brannon brothers as they got out of the wagon. Dead or alive, it didn't make any difference as far as the bounty was concerned. He briefly admired the beauty of Verna Conmy as her husband and the big Light Horseman handed her down to the ground, but he hardly gave a second thought to the two young sportsmen. City dudes, thinking to go outlaw-hunting for sport! The notion would have been laughable if Sid Gifford had been in the mood for laughing.

As it was, his whole mind was on the job ahead. Lord, he thought quietly to himself, how sick I am of being a lawman! Dollar a day and ten-cent mileage. Sleeping in the weather, riding when you're sick.

Well, no more of that after today. No more of that!

Some forty yards behind the marshal, Duane Keating idly aimed his rifle at the back of Gifford's head. But he wasn't really interested in the marshal—not at the moment, anyway. As the wagons began to unload at the entrance to the graveyard, he found another target. The sights rested steadily on the center of Warren Conmy's cord jacket.

CHAPTER TWELVE

Beeler did not spot the three possemen until the service was almost over. The two known as Roy and Brian had stationed themselves in the thick of the Indians. The third posseman was standing a little behind Beeler, ready to cut off any try for escape in that direction. There they stood, hats in their hands, their eyes slightly glazed as they waited patiently for Duel Hooker to wind up his prayer. There was not much to set them apart from the Indians who surrounded them. Their sun-darkened faces might have been Creek faces, or half-blood at the very least. The thing that set them apart, and the thing that Beeler finally noticed, was the give-away bulge of their revolvers.

Beeler's first reaction was one of anger. Anger at George Forestman for tricking him. At Preacher Hooker for failing to support him. But after a moment he shrugged the anger away. He glanced at the two Brannon brothers and sighed to himself. "Maybe my mistake was trying to help you in the first place," he thought. Well, it didn't matter now. The game was over—for them, as well as for Conmy and Sutter.

One of the possemen—the one called Milo—was looking at Beeler now. He grinned and shook his head; a warning more eloquent than words. The wise gambler knew when the cards were falling against him; it was time for Beeler to get out of the game. Time to let the Brannons take care of themselves.

Some of Beeler's unrest must have shown on his face, for Babe Brannon was scowling and looking at him doubtfully. "What's the matter?" he hissed from the side of his mouth.

With a little shrug of surrender, Beeler said, "I think the game's about over. You and Leo had better cash in while you're still alive."

The outlaw stared at him. "What're you talkin' about?"

"Somewhere along the line, three federal possemen mixed in with the funeral crowd. The marshal's down there by the river, coverin' the affair with his rifle."

Babe shot several wild glances around at the silent crowd. "I don't see anybody."

"They're here all the same. You and Leo haven't got a chance now. Against Conmy and Sutter you might just have made it, but not any more. When the possemen throw down on you, my advice is to give up."

The almost silent but excited exchange had caught Leo's attention. He nudged Beeler. "What's all the talk about?"

Beeler sighed. "See the man over there?" He glanced at Milo. "He's a federal posseman. And there are two others. The marshal is down by the river keepin' watch with a rifle."

Leo shot an anxious look in Milo's direction. "How do you know?"

"It used to be my business to know such things. Take my word for it."

The outlaw took a deep breath and made a hard decision. "We'll just have to fight our way out of here."

"You wouldn't have a chance," Beeler told him wearily.

"I ain't goin' to no federal prison for the rest of my natural life. Maybe even get myself hung." Leo shook his head angrily. "No, sir, that ain't for Leo Brannon."

"Start a fuss while the funeral's goin' on," Beeler told him coldly, "and the Indians will have your hide. If Conmy and Sutter and the lawmen don't get it first."

"I ain't goin' to no prison," Leo said again. "I just ain't, and that's all there is to it." He looked at his brother. "Babe?"

Babe made a vague sound of anger. "I guess we ain't got much to lose."

Up on the slope Milo was beginning to look alarmed. He caught the attention of the other two possemen, and they began to slowly close in on either side of the outlaws.

By this time Conmy and Sutter had sensed the desperation in the air. They shot inquiring glances at each other, then at Beeler and the outlaws.

"What do you think?" Conmy asked with a glance.

Sutter looked at the outlaws. "I think they're about to make a break for it."

"Before the funeral's over?"

"I guess they've decided it doesn't make much difference whether we kill them, or the Indians. Either way, they're dead."

Conmy thought about this for a moment. "Nothing has changed," he said quietly. "The game is still on. Agreed?"

Sutter shrugged. "Of course."

"Equal points for Beeler and Babe Brannon. One additional point for Leo Brannon, because he's the leader of the gang."

Sutter nodded. "Agreed, but there's nothing we can do about it now. Without guns."

Conmy glared angrily but had to agree. "All right, if they do make a break, we'll head for the river and get rifles and horses from Keating and O'Toole."

It was then that Leo Brannon hauled the heavy .45 out of his waistband where it had been hiding beneath his left arm. Frank Beeler groaned and cursed himself for allowing Leo to smuggle the revolver out of the camp house.

For a moment Conmy and Sutter did nothing. They stared in disbelief as the two outlaws charged directly at them across the grassy slope. Wide-eyed, Conmy tried to shove his wife out of the way. Sutter, acting on instinct, threw himself at Babe.

Perhaps Leo believed that Sutter was going after a hidden weapon of his own. He wheeled suddenly and pointed the revolver at Sutter, and within a matter of seconds the young huntsman was dead. The pistol bellowed. Ben Sutter took a step back in astonishment and then fell with a splash of crimson blood on the brown grass.

Verna screamed. Babe quickly grabbed her in one bearlike arm and used her as a shield as he and Leo began backing away.

At the open grave, Brother Duel Hooker had finished his prayer. The pallbearers had lowered the small casket into the grave; the gravediggers had scooped red dirt into their shovels and were passing it around to the Forestman family. First the Forestmans, then their friends, accepted bits of dirt and dropped it into the grave. Until the moment that Leo leveled the revolver at Sutter and fired, only a few of the Indians had been aware of any disturbance.

Marshal Sid Gifford, his rifle resting casually in the fork of a young cottonwood, stared in disbelief as the madness around the grave began to develop. The Indians were still passing quietly in front of the grave, dropping in little clods of earth. Most of them stopped to shake hands with the old parson and the preacher, as well as the male members of the Forestman family. Some of them had already started for the hitching ground to get their teams. Marshal Gifford watched it all with the cool self-assurance of a man who had been allowed a glimpse into the immediate future and thoroughly approved of what he saw. The funeral was, at long last, drawing to an end. Soon the Brannons—and the bounty—would be his. The lawman smiled to himself. That was when the two outlaws suddenly began racing along the slope in the general direction of the hitching ground.

It seemed almost by accident that they ran headlong into the two dudes. Conmy looked stunned at first, as if a rabbit that he had been pursuing had suddenly turned to the attack. Sutter's face was impassive; he sized the situation up in a second and recognized it for what it was.

Gifford realized that the Brannons, at the last moment, had decided on this desperate action of their own. They had flung aside any chance of help from the Indians, and they had cut loose from Beeler. Leo and Babe Brannon had simply decided that they would rather settle their destiny on the spot than to worry about it later in a federal prison.

Before the marshal could fire, or even line up his target, the Indians began to mill in alarm. A broad Creek face reared up suddenly between Gifford and the outlaws. In the meantime Ben Sutter had made a decision of his own, throwing himself at the lead outlaw. That was when Leo

Brannon raised his pistol and fired into the young man's face.

For a moment Gifford lost track of all that was going on. Some of the Creeks were beginning to shout in their excitement and anger. "Goddammit, Roy, Brian, where are you?" the lawman snarled to himself. He could feel that bounty money dribbling through his fingers like river sand. For an instant he caught a glimpse of Milo, who seemed stunned and helpless by this sudden turn of events, but the other two possemen were lost somewhere in the churning mass of excited Indians.

Gifford didn't waste a split second in grieving for the dead Sutter. He and his pal had come looking for adventure and excitement—well, they had found it. For a moment the marshal had Babe Brannon in his sights, but before there was a chance of dropping him, the outlaw had grabbed Verna Conmy.

Suddenly the scene was frozen.

Appalled, the Indians stared at the dead man, at Leo Brannon with the smoking pistol in his hand, at Babe Brannon who had the hysterical Verna Conmy locked in one arm.

Warren Conmy's face was as pale as calf tallow. He stared for an instant at his dead brother-in-law. He wheeled to look into his wife's terror-filled eyes. Suddenly he didn't know what to do. Gods had fallen; devils now controlled the world that had once belonged to the Conmys and Sutters.

Verna cried, “Warren, help me!”

Like a man caught in the grip of a nightmare, Conmy threw himself at Babe Brannon. By that time one of Gifford’s possemen had drawn his revolver and was firing wildly. Leo, on the verge of hysteria, was hollering, “Ever’body stay where you are! We’re backin’ out of here and you can get on with your funeral!” he glared at Beeler. “You, too, Marshal! From here on out, me and Babe looks out for ourselves!”

“You won’t even make it to the river,” Beeler told him angrily.

“Maybe. But we aim to give it the best try we know how. Now rustle them possemen all together in a bunch. Get their guns and throw them over here.”

Beeler started to shake his head in refusal. But he changed his mind and motioned to the possemen. As they talked angrily of matters of life and death, Verna Conmy screamed and fought hysterically against Babe’s ironlike hug. Not many seemed to notice that Warren Conmy had fallen in the sudden burst of gunfire and now lay dead only a few yards from his brother-in-law.

From his position in the brush, some forty yards in back of Marshal Sid Gifford, Duane Keating watched the beginning of the bizarre scene in the graveyard. He gripped his rifle so hard that his arms began to ache. The sights had found the center of Babe Brannon's forehead, but he did not dare to fire as long as the outlaw had Verna in his grasp. The sights moved for a moment from the outlaw to Warren Conmy. He experienced a fierce satisfaction at Warren's look of helplessness.

Keating spared himself a glance at the dead form of Ben Sutter. Everything had happened so fast; he felt slightly dizzy. Ben dead. Warren helpless, unable to act, even as his wife cried for help. Well, the secretary thought grimly, maybe now Verna would see her husband as he really was.

He dragged his attention back to Marshal Gifford. The lawman was angrily tracking the action in the graveyard over the sights of his rifle. Almost irresistibly, the muzzle of Keating's own rifle drifted toward the marshal. A thought, deadly and full grown, rose up in his mind. *If Warren Conmy were to suddenly die with a rifle bullet in his heart, who could say that Keating had fired the shot and not Gifford?*

The answer was coldly obvious: No one. In all the excitement, the lawman had simply made a mistake and killed the wrong man.

Keating realized that there would be questions in the minds of some—but would it really matter, if the marshal were not alive to answer them for himself? Keating quickly decided that it wouldn't.

Leo and Babe began working their way toward the hitching ground, with Verna sobbing in Babe's arms. Captain George Forestman, his face almost black with outrage, started toward them. Leo hollered at him and waved his pistol. "Don't stir, Cap'n, or I'll kill you! Light Horse or not, I'll kill you!"

Beeler heard the shrill edge of hysteria in the outlaw's voice and was relieved to see Forestman stop in his tracks. Somewhere in the crowd a young girl began to cry, but most of the Creek women were as suddenly silent as stone statues. They glared at the whites in hatred, but at the moment they made no move to intervene. Maybe, Beeler thought to himself, the Brannons would make it as far as the hitching ground. With horses, maybe they'd even make it to the river. But no farther. The marshal, then O'Toole or Keating. If not them, the Indians.

Beeler called angrily to the posseman known as Milo. "How many men has the marshal got at the river?"

The posseman threw his hands in the air with disgust. "Nobody. Just hisself, that is. He said he'd cover us with his rifle if a commotion started. Some cover!"

"Didn't you find the two riflemen that Conmy and Sutter stationed down there?"

"Just one. A peg-legged bird with a face like a side of beef. Roy knocked him on the head with his Winchester, and we left him where he fell."

Leo and Babe were now at the hitching ground.

Still using Verna Conmy as a shield, they disappeared into the mass of animals and wagons. Within a matter of seconds Babe had flung Verna aside; they mounted the horses that Duel Hooker had staked out for them and streaked for the timber in a cloud of red dust.

Beeler observed it all with an almost overwhelming indifference. No longer did he bother himself about the two outlaws. George Forestman and a dozen other Creek men were already quietly rounding up saddle animals. They would take care of the Brannons. Federal laws or no federal laws, this time they would take care of their own problems. So the Brannons, as far as Beeler was concerned, could go to hell—and probably would—his one thought at the moment was for Duane Keating.

"Milo," Beeler said, "you and the others stay here and look after Mrs. Conmy. I guess there's nothin' we can do about her husband and brother right now except drag them back from the Forestman grave." He turned and walked off toward the river. As he walked he heard the gravediggers filling the grave. None of the Indians looked in his direction. Once Beeler glanced at Brother Duel Hooker, but the preacher's face was as cold and expressionless as a slab of granite.

"Well," Beeler thought resignedly, "I can give up any notion of ever ridin' for the federal court again." His days in Indian Territory were over.

• • •

Humphrey O'Toole was sitting on the ground at the edge of the timber, with Marshal Gifford's rifle at his side. His hair was matted with blood, and fat, bitter tears streamed down his beef-red face. He looked up at Beeler. "I ought to get up from here," he said in a voice choked with grief and bitterness. "Mrs. Conmy will need me now. But somehow I can't seem to make myself move."

"Where's Keating?"

The butler raised a hand and dumbly indicated the dense brush near the river.

Keating was dead, as Beeler had known he would be. Shot through the chest by the marshal's rifle, but by O'Toole's hand. Beeler returned to where the butler was still sitting and found Marshal Sid Gifford, also dead, in a patch of mullein.

"Who killed the marshal?"

O'Toole made a meaningless gesture with his hands. "Keating. First he killed the marshal, then Mr. Conmy."

His lawman's instinct prompted Beeler to retrace his steps, from Keating to Gifford to O'Toole. In his mind he pieced together the story. Keating, for whatever dark reasons he might have had, had killed Conmy during the posseman's outburst of pistol fire. Then probably with the intention of claiming that the marshal had shot Conmy by mistake, Keating had killed the marshal.

Keating had also intended to kill O'Toole, but somewhere along the line the butler had regained consciousness and spoiled Keating's plans.

Beeler returned to the butler who was now trying to shove himself off the ground. "Give me a hand, Beeler. I've got to go to Mrs. Conmy."

"Gifford's possemen are lookin' after her now."

"Nevertheless, I must go. It's my duty."

Beeler held out a hand and pulled him off the ground. "Why did Keating kill Warren Conmy?"

O'Toole shot him a look of bitterness and hatred. "You traveled with them, saw them together. Don't you know?"

Beeler sighed. "I guess I do." As the butler began stumping up the grade to the graveyard, Beeler called, "Tell Mrs. Conmy that I'm sorry, but she'll have to stay nearby until another deputy marshal gets on the job."

"How long will that be?"

"A long time, maybe, if the Creeks kill the Brannons when they catch them. Not so long, if they decide to let the court have them."

He built a cigarette and sat on a log and smoked it, and he made a point of not looking at the dead marshal. He watched as the Indians hurriedly left the graveyard. Within a few minutes all wagons and animals were off the hitching ground. Verna Conmy and O'Toole and the three possemen had moved out of the graveyard, the dead men had been laid out behind a gravehouse, conveniently out of sight. Verna Conmy was sitting on the ground holding her face in her hands, and Beeler supposed that she was crying. But he didn't really care.

Lord, he thought wearily, it seems like a hundred years since we pulled out of Oklahoma City—Frank Beeler with thoughts of renewed credit and successful homesteads in his head! How many days had it been? He couldn't remember. But in all that time he had hardly given Elizabeth Stans even a passing thought.

Now he did think about her, absently, and without emotion. As a farmer, he was a failure. As a federal lawman he was through, because the Indians were through with him. "I'm a poor prospect for marriage, Elizabeth," he thought, "and I don't think I'll go into it any time soon." When Elizabeth heard the whole story, he didn't think that she would mind.

After an hour O'Toole returned and wanted to know if he could take Verna back to camp. "All right," Beeler said, "but stay there until a marshal comes."

He didn't go with them because he was sick to death of the Sutters and the Conmys. So he sat there beside the dead marshal, his mind drifting aimlessly. After a while the three possemen—perfect pictures of frustration and disgust at having lost out on the Brannon bounty money—came to join him. Once, near sundown, they heard a spatter of rifleshots from far downstream.

“Well, that ends it,” one of the possemen said and spat on the ground.

Shortly before nightfall Captain Forestman’s party returned, and Beeler noted without interest that they had taken the Brannons alive. The two outlaws were almost overcome with frustration and self-pity.

“Look,” Leo said anxiously to Beeler, “these Indians is friends of yours, ain’t they? Talk to them and make them let us go! Hell, we ain’t done anything to the Indians; and they don’t give a damn if a couple of white men get killed in a little shootin’ scrape.”

Beeler was singularly unmoved by the outlaws’ whining. The temptation to lecture and rail at them was strong, but in the end he only said, “Leo, you and Babe never should of left the farm.”